Bearly Human

Ferguson Ray

Pepperback Press, Inc.

One

Friday, August 29, 2025

Engines sing when they're in tune. When everything is all lined up and running smoothly, the music of hundreds of metal parts sings in perfect harmony. But when an engine falls out of alignment, the melody sours. An out of tune engine scrapes across my brain like nails on a chalkboard.

It only takes one bad part to ruin the song of an engine. Lives are like that, too.

The bolt under my wrench gave a satisfying click as it snugged into place, and I slid out from beneath Mrs. Peterson's ancient Volvo. The odors of burnt metal, motor oil, and the lingering ghost of the tuna sandwich Quinn had eaten for lunch several hours ago permeated the garage. That combination had become oddly comforting over the past couple of months.

"Done," I announced, levering myself up from the creeper.

"You're a freaking miracle worker, Harper," Quinn said, appearing at my side like a ninja. Her red curls were escaping their ponytail prison in every direction, making her look like she'd stuck her finger in an electrical socket. "Dad swore that transmission was ready for the junkyard."

"You scared the shit out of me," I scolded her for the millionth time, blowing the bangs that had escaped my French braid out of my eyes. "You've got to stop sneaking up on me while I'm holding really big wrenches." I placed the tool in question back in its slot and wiped my grease-stained hands on an equally grease-stained rag.

"Mrs. Peterson can't afford a whole new transmission and she definitely doesn't have new-car money." I gave up and tossed the rag onto my workbench and arched an eyebrow at Quinn. "Your dad underestimated my stubbornness."

Quinn grinned and stood on tiptoe to tuck my annoying bangs behind my ear. "My hero. Speaking of which, a bunch of us are heading to Rusty's tonight. It's Taco Tuesday and they have dangerously strong margaritas."

"Pass." The word shot out of my mouth faster than a speeding bullet.

"Harp, come on. It's time to get back on the horse. You can't hide forever."

"I'm not hiding. I'm...strategically avoiding situations that involve men and tequila." I unzipped my coveralls and stepped out of the legs, revealing the ripped knees of my jeans.

"It's been three months since you escaped Douchebag Derek. You're allowed to have fun again." Quinn leaned against the workbench, her expression softening. "This is a really nice group. Just come out and eat some cheap mozzarella sticks with us."

I almost caved. The hopeful look in my best friend's eyes was nearly impossible to resist. But the memory of Derek's voice slithered through my mind: You're not going out dressed like that, are you?

"Rain check," I said, forcing a smile. "I wanted to take a walk along the boardwalk tonight. It's so peaceful now that some of the summer traffic is starting to die down."

Quinn sighed dramatically. "Fine. But don't stay out too late, it's going to rain. Buckets. Torrential. Biblical proportions."

I glanced out the garage's open bay door at the perfectly clear blue sky. "Where did you hear that?"

"My elbows. And they never lie," she said with theatrical seriousness. "These joints have predicted three hurricanes and the great flood of 2017."

"You're too young to have weather-predicting joints," I said, grabbing my jacket from the hook and throwing it over my plain tee. "Tell your dad I'll see him bright and early tomorrow morning."

"Your funeral," Quinn called after me as I walked out. "Don't come crying to me when you're swept out to sea!"

Weathered wood creaked beneath my sneakers and the waves rumbled gently as they rolled in and out against the empty beach. In September, Santa Paola had slipped into its annual state of off-season hibernation. The sun-seekers were all safely back in the city for the winter and this late in the day, even the locals had abandoned the boardwalk. It was just me and the endless blue of the ocean stretching toward the horizon.

Three months ago, I'd shown up on Quinn's doorstep with a black eye, a duffel bag full of tools, and an empty bank account. Thanks to her and her dad, I was starting over with a good job that I loved. They'd even helped me find the little cottage I was renting and I was slowly rebuilding my life.

Progress. Slow, painful progress.

The wind picked up, carrying the scents of salt and seaweed. I pulled my jacket tighter and kept walking, passing shuttered ice cream shops and souvenir stands, their cheerful signs faded from decades of exposure.

The sun was dipping down toward the horizon, and a flash of light at my feet brought me to a stop. A coin winked up at me, bright against the greyed wood of the boardwalk.

"What have we here?" I murmured, squatting down to pick it up.

The coin was copper like a penny, but much larger and thicker. Straightening, I ran my thumb over the embossed logo and brought the coin closer to get a better look. The central shape was an eye, surrounded by block lettering, *Your Adventure Awaits*.

"Cool." This must be some kind of token for one of the arcades or rides on the boardwalk. The eye logo was kind of familiar. I couldn't quite place it, but everything was closed now anyway.

I moved to slip the coin into my pocket, absently searching the signs above the gated businesses, when my gaze landed on a couple of ancient carnival games tucked under a low awning. I'd passed this spot a dozen times during my evening walks but had never noticed them before. The one on the left housed a dusty mannequin dressed as a fortune teller sitting before a deck of cards. The other was an old-fashioned claw machine full of stuffed toys.

The claw machine beckoned with a bright green light over its coin slot.

"Weird," I whispered, moving closer like a moth to a flame.

The machine looked straight out of the 1950s, with faded red paint over its metal frame and a large mechanical claw. Inside, instead of the usual collection of cheap stuffed animals, there were what appeared to be vintage articulated teddy bears in a variety of hues. One was pressed up against the glass, with dark brown fur and round green glass eyes.

"Hey, handsome," I said, tapping the glass. "You're looking a little lonely in there."

At the base of the machine was a token slot with a faded instruction: "ONE TOKEN, ONE CHANCE."

I looked at the coin in my palm. The token looked like it would fit the slot perfectly.

"What do I have to lose?" I muttered, sliding the token in before I could overthink it.

Lights flickered to life across the machine's facade and a smooth, bassy hum erupted from deep within the metal casing. I wrapped my hands around the hard rubber joystick, and the vibration sent tingles up my arms. With barely a nudge from me, the claw moved to hover over the bear with the green eyes. The controls went lax in my hand as the automation took over. The purr of the machine's hidden gears changed, the octave seeming to rise with excitement as the claw descended and long metal fingers reached out for the bear. They grasped it firmly around the middle, and—miracle of miracles—actually picked it up.

"No way," I breathed as the claw deposited the teddy into the prize chute. I reached in and pulled out my prize.

The toy was surprisingly heavy, with soft, textured fur and those striking glass eyes. A tiny silver tag hung from its ear with an embroidered name: "Ronan."

"Ronan, huh?" I held the bear up to eye level. "Nice to meet you. I'm Harper."

A deafening crack of thunder sent me spinning around. The sky, which had been perfectly clear five minutes ago, was now completely dark, with a haze of clouds obscuring the moon. Fat droplets of rain splashed onto the boardwalk, leaving dark circles on the dry wood.

Quinn's stupid elbows had been right.

"Damn it!" I huddled under the overhang as the darkened pattern left by the raindrops melted together. In seconds, the walkway was drenched and I was trapped.

"Damn," I repeated flatly, resigned to my fate. I was about to get wet, but hopefully I could save my new friend. I tucked the bear under my jacket and zipped it up. With his firm weight against me, I sprinted down the boardwalk.

I was immediately soaked.

My cottage sat a quarter-mile from the beach, a tiny blue saltbox that was charming in better weather. Right now, it looked like heaven. I fumbled with my keys, cursing as the rain plastered my hair to my face and my clothes to my skin.

Finally pushing inside, I slammed the door behind me and leaned back against it, dripping onto the cheerful little rug I'd picked up at the local flea market. As my heartbeat slowed, I unzipped my jacket and inspected my prize.

"You okay in there, little guy?" I smoothed down his ruffled fur, which was only a little damp around the edges. "Quinn is never going to let me hear the end of this."

I carried Ronan the Teddy Bear into the bathroom and set him on the counter. The sound of rain hammered against the roof, punctuated by occasional claps of thunder that rocked the tiny house.

"Don't look," I joked to the bear as I pulled my wet t-shirt over my head. His button eyes glinted in the bathroom light. "This is already more action than I've had in months."

Worried that the power might go out at any moment, I took out my braid and hopped into the shower. I let myself bask in the heat for a couple of minutes, then quickly washed my hair. Rinsing off, I pulled back the curtain to find the bear's flat plastic eyes staring intently into the distance.

"Close your eyes," I told him, reaching for a towel.

The absurdity hit me, and I snorted. "And this is exactly what happens when you move to a town where you only know one person and you refuse to socialize. You end up having conversations with inanimate objects."

Once dried and changed into sweatpants and an oversized t-shirt that read MECHANICS DO IT WITH TOOLS, I carried the bear into the living room. The cottage was small but cozy, with mismatched furniture and a comfortable overstuffed couch I'd rescued from the curb.

I settled into the soft cushions, tucked my feet under me, and propped Ronan against the armrest so he was facing me. The rain continued its assault outside, the muffled roar creating a comforting backdrop.

"So, Ronan the Teddy Bear," I said, pulling a throw blanket over my legs, "welcome to Casa Harper. It's not much, but it's mine—well, my name is on the lease—and it's douchebag-free, which is the important part."

The bear's green eyes caught the warm light from my reading lamp.

"Douchebag Derek was my ex," I explained, as if the bear had asked. "We met our last year of college. Classic tale—boy meets girl, boy sweeps girl off her feet, boy turns into controlling asshole." I twisted a strand of long brown hair around my finger.

Thunder rumbled outside, and I pulled the blanket higher.

"The funny thing is," I murmured, "I'm a mechanic. I fix things for a living. Engines make sense to me—they have clear problems with clear solutions." I gave the bear a sad smile. "People? Not so much. I didn't see the warning light with Derek until it was almost too late."

I ran a hand over the bear's rough fur. "You're a good listener, Ronan. Better than Quinn, who just wants me to get back on the horse."

The bear sat silently, his expression unchanging but somehow sympathetic.

"And I know she's right, so you don't have to say it," I said, poking him gently in the belly. "Quinn may sound like a ditz, but she can see right through people." I stared into the distance. "I'm working on it."

I scooped up the bear and held him against my chest, his soft fur tickling my chin. A peculiar warmth seemed to radiate from him, almost like a heartbeat.

"I used to be a hugger," I murmured into the top of his head. "Congrats, Ronan. You're the first male I've touched in three months, and you're not even human."

Another crash of thunder, closer this time, made me jump. The lights flickered ominously.

"Great," I muttered. "Okay, Harper, time to stop talking to stuffed animals and go to bed."

I stood up, cradling the bear in my arms, and walked through the tiny house, checking that the doors and each window were locked tight before heading toward the bedroom. Rain continued to lash against the windows, and the wind howled through the eaves of my little cottage. In the bedroom, I turned off the overhead light, leaving just a small nightlight burning on my nightstand.

Slipping under the quilted comforter, I set the bear on the bed beside me. Without conscious thought, my hand slid under my pillow to touch the cold metal of the wrench tucked beneath it.

"You know what, buddy?" I yawned, arranging myself on my side and smiling blearily as the storm's white noise lulled me toward sleep. "Tonight might be the first night I don't have bad dreams. Wouldn't that be nice?"

TWO

Ronan

"You worry too much, Ro," Tommy called out from where he was constructing a massive sand castle with turrets at each corner. "Everything is going to be fine."

I kept my eyes closed and didn't respond. Out of all of us, Tommy was the one who really had his shit together. He'd finished school and had a good job set up for September. But none of the others seemed worried either. The rushing of the waves nearly drowned out their carefree voices. Music played on Sean's old transistor radio, the melody drifting in and out like the tide.

Maybe they were right, maybe I worried too much.

I stretched out on the old blanket we always brought to the beach, letting the warmth of the sand beneath it unknot my muscles one by one. The sound of the ocean pulled at me, trying to drag me under into sleep. Tommy was smart. He was probably right. I could afford to relax, just for today.

My thoughts began to drift, becoming hazy and disconnected. The memory of a woman's voice whispered on the edge of my consciousness, soft and sweet. The roar of the waves became the patter of rain against a roof.

You're a good listener, Ronan, she murmured, and my name on her lips sent electricity down my spine.

Tonight might be the first night I don't have bad dreams...

My eyes snapped open.

The sound of water still crashed around me, but it was dark. I held perfectly still as my mind struggled up through the layers of my dream. I was no longer on that sun-drenched beach. Instead, I was lying in a bed, a small nightlight casting a faint warm glow over the far end of the strange room while a storm raged outside.

I didn't recognize the bed, the room, or the woman lying next to me.

Angling my body away from the lithe brunette cuddled against me, I tried to get a look at her face. Perfect pale skin ran over the strong curve of her jaw and continued up to high cheekbones. My gaze lingered on the dark circles nearly hidden by her long, dark lashes, and my heart squeezed.

Harper.

Memories came rushing back at me. Lying on the beach in the sun with Sean and our friends...that was so long ago. Another lifetime. Years spent frozen, watching the world pass me by. Then, last night, *Harper.*

Another crack of thunder shook the tiny cottage and she stirred beside me, her long legs brushing against mine. For the first time in years—decades, really—my body stirred. Sensation and blood rushed through me and I took a long, deep breath. My lungs filled with

Harper's sweet, clean scent, which didn't help calm down some parts of me at all.

Her fingers twitched against my chest, and I froze. The simple touch sent sparks dancing across my skin. Harper was wearing a top of some kind, but I was completely, totally naked.

I should get out of this bed. Run down to the board-walk and bust open that machine. Figure out how I was going to explain all of this. Find clothes. Maybe not in that order. But I should definitely do something other than lie here next to this beautiful woman who had no idea what she'd brought into her bed.

I didn't.

The storm continued its assault outside while Harper slept peacefully beside me, her breath warming my shoulder in a steady rhythm. When was the last time I'd felt someone's breath against my skin?

She shifted closer, seeking heat in her sleep. The rush of sensation was almost painful after so long. I gritted my teeth and tried to think about anything else. Motorcycle engines. Oil changes. That time Tommy dropped the engine from his 1951 Chief on my foot.

It didn't help.

Harper made a small sound in her throat and pressed her face into my neck. My arms moved of their own accord, wrapping around her. She fit against me perfectly, like she'd been made to sleep in my embrace.

She relaxed into my arms, totally trusting in her sleep. The weight of that trust settled over me like a warm blanket. This woman had rescued me, brought me into her home, confided her fears. She deserved better than to wake up to a strange naked man in her bed.

But I couldn't leave her. Not now. Not ever. The moment she pulled me out of the machine, I felt it. The spark. The connection.

Now, holding her close while rain drummed against the roof, I knew with bone-deep certainty that she was the answer I'd been waiting for all these years.

My eyes grew heavy as her warmth seeped into my skin. I knew I should stay awake and figure out how to explain all this to her in the morning. But the steady sound of her breathing and the gentle rise and fall of her chest against mine pulled me under.

For the first time in years, I drifted off to sleep feeling completely, wonderfully human.

Harper

Warmth enveloped me, radiating from a solid mass pressed against my side. There was smooth skin under my fingertips and a spicy, masculine scent filled my nose. My dream lover smelled like motor oil, leather, and a storm rolling in off the ocean.

My body melted into his delicious heat. God, I needed this. How long had it been since I'd been held like this? How long had it been since someone had touched me and I'd felt safe?

I tried to cling to the oblivion of sleep, but the faint vibration of my phone against the nightstand was pulling me away. In just a minute my second alarm would go off, shattering this lovely dream.

As much as I wished I could lay here in the dark, fantasizing about some perfect dream lover, I was lucky to have the job at Quinn's dad's garage, and I needed to get my ass out of bed. I sighed and reached out to grab the phone. As I leaned forward, the heat at my back shifted, and I froze.

There was someone in my bed.

Ice replaced the warmth in my veins as reality crashed in. Derek. He'd found me. My body froze as panic rushed through me, along with memories of our last encounter. The black eye had healed months ago, but suddenly my orbital bone ached as if it had just happened. In a split second, I relived the moment when Derek's bluster had become a punch.

Never again.

My hand slid under my pillow and wrapped around the hardened steal of my favorite wrench. My dad had given it to me at 16, along with my first old beater car. *A tool like this isn't just for fixing things*, he'd told me with a wink. I'd hefted the solid shape in my hand and looked up at him in confusion. *It can break them, too.*

Moving slowly, I levered my body away from the form behind me, twisting as I rose to a sitting position, wrench firmly in hand.

My racing heartbeat stuttered as I took in the outline of the man beside me. It was still dark, but...but that...that wasn't Derek.

Dark hair, sharp jawline. A tattoo curved around his bicep, the black ink stark against tan skin.

A tattoo? Derek would never. Now that I was fully awake, I realized the scent was wrong, too. My ex had always smelled like expensive cologne and cigarettes.

Relief hit me like a shot of tequila, hot and dizzying. Derek hadn't found me. I was safe.

Wait. No. I was not safe. The guy sleeping in my bed was gorgeous--all lean muscle and tattoos—but he was still a stranger. A naked stranger.

From what I could make out in the darkness, he was also completely asleep, his face peaceful, full lips slightly parted. I kept trying to talk myself back into being scared. There was a strange nude man in my bed. But my brain kept circling back to: *Not Derek. Not Derek. Not Derek.*

The stranger's chest rose and fell in steady breaths.

Focus, Harper. Strange naked man equals danger.

I turned on the small lamp on my bedside table and soft light flooded the room. Now that I could see the man in my bed more clearly, I was even more confused.

Why was there a hot biker god in my bed?

The man's eyes drifted open, startling green.

"Harper," he sighed.

His voice jolted through me like I'd touched a live wire. "How do you know my name?" I demanded. I didn't give him a chance to answer. "Get the fuck out of my house!"

The man held up a large hand with thick, tapered fingers and scrambled backward. He slid off the bed, taking the cover with him.

The wrench left my hand in a perfect arc, connecting with a solid thunk as he disappeared over the side of the bed.

"Ha!" I scrambled to my knees. "That's what you get for breaking into my house, you naked weirdo!"

Silence.

"Hello?" I called out, heart pounding. "Naked guy?"

Nothing.

Moving carefully to the edge of the bed, I peered over.

The comforter was strewn across the floor. I scrambled off of the bed and grabbed at the blanket, whipping it up. Beneath it was my trusty wrench...and Ronan the Teddy Bear.

"Huh." I grabbed the wrench and collapsed back onto the bed, heart still pounding. "What the hell?"

The heavy metal tool was cool and solid in my hand—definitely real. But the rest?

Quinn's voice echoed in my head, *You can't hide forever.*

"Fine," I muttered to the ceiling. "Next time she invites me out, I'll go. Clearly, I need more human interaction before I completely lose it."

I reached down and scooped up the bear, straightening his little arm. His green glass eyes caught the lamplight as I set him on the nightstand.

"No offense Ronan, but I think I need to start talking to actual humans again."

Three

The garage was empty but the morning sun streamed through the open bay doors, and the fresh scent of coffee filled the interior. I weaved my way through the cars in various stages of disassembly to the small kitchenette. Sitting the teddy bear on the counter, I poured myself a nice full mug and raised it to my lips to take my first sip of the morning.

"Who's your friend?" Quinn's voice chirped from behind me.

I jumped, spilling scalding hot coffee across my chest. "What did we say about the ninja routine?" I snapped, grabbing paper towels and blotting at the wet stains now dotting my white t-shirt.

"Sorry about your boobs!" Quinn sang out and pointed at Ronan. "Seriously though, introduce me to your handsome little friend."

I sighed and tossed the wet paper towels into the trash. "This is Ronan." I walked him over to my workbench and made him a clean spot where he'd have a view of the entire garage. "I figured he could be my new assistant, since he's better qualified than most of the guys who've applied here."

"As long as he's house-trained." Quinn, who had followed us over, snatched Ronan from the bench and held him up to her face, examining him closely. "Where'd you get him?"

"The old claw machine on the boardwalk." I stepped into my coveralls and zipped them over my coffee-stained t-shirt. "Right before your demon elbows summoned that storm."

"Told you so." Quinn's eyes narrowed. "Wait, you won something from a claw machine? Seriously?"

"Maybe my luck is changing." I plucked him out of her hands, running my hands over his fur, and put him back in his spot. "Though I did have the weirdest dream last night..."

"Ooooh, do tell." Quinn hopped up onto my workbench beside the bear, swinging her legs.

I sighed and girded my loins. "There was a guy—"

"A guy?" Quinn's eyebrows shot up.

"—in my bed—"

"In your bed!?" she parroted, an octave higher.

"—naked."

"Holy crap!" She clasped her hands in joy, bouncing on the bench.

I held up a hand. "Calm down. It was a dream," I reminded her. "Geez. I'm not that bad, am I?"

Quinn nodded her head in an exaggerated motion. "You are. You really are." She clapped her hands again, flapping her dangling feet like a toddler. "Tell me everything," she insisted.

"Really, that was kind of the whole gist of it." I shrugged and began setting out my tools for the day.

She frowned at me. "Start with what he looked like."

"Tall, dark, and handsome," I admitted. "Tattoos."

"Oooh, exactly the opposite of Douchebag Derek. Your subconscious has excellent taste." Quinn waggled her eyebrows. "Did he say anything?"

I hesitated, my hand hovering over a socket. I could see his full lips moving, his green eyes locked on mine. "He said my name."

"Awww, that's so sweet," Quinn cooed. "And did he boink your brains out?"

Heat crept up my neck. "We were just cuddling."

"Harper Brinkman, you slut!" She offered me a high five, which I reluctantly returned. "This is awesome. Your brain is clearly trying to tell you something. Like maybe it's time to—"

"If you say 'get back on the horse,' I will throw this wrench at you." I paused, memories sparking. "Actually, I did that in the dream, too."

"You threw a wrench at me in your dream?" Quinn asked with mock offense.

I rolled my eyes. "Not you, the naked guy."

Quinn smacked her hand against her forehead. "You've forgotten what naked men in your bed are for! I know it's only been three months, but that's like a decade in vagina years."

"Morning, girls." Frank's gruff voice made us both jump. Quinn's dad stood in the doorway to his office, coffee mug in hand. His eyes fixed on Ronan for a long moment before sliding away. "Is Mrs. Peterson's paperwork ready?"

"Yup." I picked up my mug from the bench and took a fortifying sip to avoid making eye contact.

He nodded, shot one more look at the bear, then disappeared back into his office without another word. I often wondered if Quinn talked so much because her dad was so quiet. Or vice versa.

The morning flew by in a blur of oil changes and brake jobs. Around noon, Mrs. Peterson bustled in wearing a hot pink velour tracksuit, a big sequined tote bag over her shoulder.

"Harper, you dear girl!" She patted at her violet-tinted hair, as if the mild autumn breeze outside had a chance against the three cans of aquanet holding her teased updo in place. "Frank tells me you worked miracles on my poor baby."

"No miracles needed, ma'am, just a few adjustments." I waved away her thanks, wiping my greasy hands on a rag. "Quinn has your paperwork at her desk."

"You're an angel, Harper. Frank is so lucky to have you." Mrs. Peterson reached out to press my hand, her grip surprisingly strong. "We all are," she said earnestly, and swept away in a cloud of gardenias and hairspray.

I was just finishing up an oil change on another car when our local computer genius rolled a muscular vintage motorcycle through the garage door, his forehead beaded with sweat and his wire-rimmed glasses slightly askew.

"Emergency!" he announced, panting over the handlebars. "I have a critical mechanical situation! I need help right now."

"What's up, Lenny?" Frank asked calmly, climbing up the metal stairs from the service pit he'd been working in. "Problem with the Triumph?"

I moved closer, admiring the perfectly restored machine. Wow. "Is that a '72?"

"It's not just a '72. It's *the* '72. And it won't start. You have to help me, Frank. This is a civic emergency. The town is counting on me to represent!"

When Frank just raised an eyebrow at him, Lenny set the bike on the kickstand and threw up his arms in exasperation.

"At the SPConCon, of course!"

I blinked and glanced over at Quinn, who shrugged. We all stared at him in silence.

"The what now?" Quinn finally asked.

"The Santa Paola Conspiracy Convention," Lenny said, pushing his glasses up. "The annual meeting of mystery enthusiasts is this weekend and this bike has its own booth and special raised viewing platform." He waved his hand grandly. "There are over two hundred people registered!" He finished with a whine.

"Right." Frank said flatly. He turned to me. "You're our resident bike expert, Harper. Can you take a look?"

"Sure. I'm done with this oil change. Let me just write up the ticket and I'll move it out back."

Within minutes I was rolling the bike up to my station. My gaze ran over the flames painted over the pristine golden to pearl white high gloss gradient on the tank and matching fenders. This was one gorgeous machine.

"You're a lifesaver." Lenny gushed, following me closely. "The disappearance of the Santa Paola Six in 1975 is what put this town on the map. My Triumph is the last remaining physical evidence we still have of their existence."

I hesitated, not wanting to encourage him, but in the end my curiosity won out. "The Santa Paola Six?" I asked.

Lenny's eyes lit up with joy as he launched into his spiel. "They were a biker gang in the 70s who disappeared without a trace. There were no bodies. No clues. They left everything behind, even their bikes."

"Interesting," I mumbled.

"Interesting? It's the greatest mystery this town has ever known!" Lenny patted the rich brown leather of the bike's seat. "All of their bikes were just sitting out there at the end of the pier the next morning. And this is the last one left. You've got to get it running. It's an important part of our history."

"I'll do my best, Lenny," I promised him. I glanced at the time and did a double take. "It's really late already, but I'll take a look first thing in the morning and give you a call, okay?"

It took some convincing, but eventually Frank was able to usher Lenny out of the garage and close up for the day. Quinn gave her dad a wave as he slipped out the door and then Quinn stood up from her desk, stretching.

"That man needs a hobby," Quinn said.

"Your dad?" I asked in confusion.

"No, I mean our resident geek, Lenny." She sidled over to me and watched as I carefully cleaned and put away my tools.

"I think his hobby may be his problem," I scoffed.

Quinn barked out a laugh. "Speaking of people who don't have a social life, want to grab dinner? I promise no tequila this time."

My stomach growled. "That sounds good."

"Victory!" She punched the air. "Let me just grab my purse."

I ran to the bathroom, taking a moment to frown at my reflection. Stained shirt? Check. No makeup? Check. Messy ponytail? Check. Yup, this was as good as it was going to get. When I came back out, Quinn was standing by the door, key in hand.

"Come on, slowpoke! I'm starving!"

It wasn't until I was home later that night, happily full of fried bar food and cheap beers, that I realized I'd left the teddy bear at the garage.

My hand actually reached for my keys before I caught myself.

"No," I told the empty room. "It's a stuffed toy." I marched myself into my bedroom and started taking off my clothes. "You're a grown woman. You do not need a security blanket."

I crawled into bed, determinedly not looking at the empty spot on my nightstand where Ronan had sat that morning. Sleep was a long time coming.

Ronan

In the blink of an eye, I was too big for the edge of Harper's workbench. My weight tipped forward, and I tumbled through the darkness, hitting the concrete floor with a thud that knocked the breath from my lungs.

"Son of a bitch," I groaned, the sound of my own voice startling.

The cold of the concrete floor seeped into my bare skin as I struggled up onto my hands and knees. Every part of me ached—from the fall, from the transformation, from fifty years of being trapped in a claw machine. I pushed myself to my feet, swaying slightly as my muscles adjusted to supporting my full height again.

The moonlight filtering through the high windows of the garage cut just enough of the darkness for me to make out the shapes of cars and workbenches. I looked down at myself—naked, just like last time. This was getting old fast.

Fifty years as a goddamn teddy bear, watching life pass me by on the boardwalk, and now...? Now I was human again two nights in a row. Why? What had changed?

Harper.

Her beautiful hazel eyes flashed across my memory, that little frown of concentration between them as she'd worked on her clients' cars all day. The way her fingers had gently straightened my arm when she'd placed me on her workbench this morning. I might not be able to move, but I could feel.

She'd called me her new assistant, with that sweet, crooked smile. The memory of it made my chest constrict.

The wind was howling again outside and the interior of the garage was way too cold to stand here naked, lost in my thoughts. I wrapped my arms around myself, looking through the dark space for something to cover up with. My gaze landed on a pair of coveralls hanging from a hook near the little back office and I padded carefully across the oil-stained concrete floor. As I slipped into the coveralls, they ended halfway down my calves, but at least I was covered. Mostly.

I turned back toward the main part of the garage and my eyes locked onto the gleaming Triumph at Harper's workstation. I still couldn't believe it.

"How are you doing, girl?" I whispered.

I circled the bike, trailing my fingers over its familiar lines. My 1972 Triumph Bonneville T120V with the custom paint job that my brother Sean had done for me as a gift for my 27th birthday. Fifty years ago.

How had she survived all these years, looking as pristine as that night I'd left her on the pier?

"What happened to you?" I murmured, kneeling beside the machine. "What the hell happened to all of us?"

I ran my hands over the gleaming tank, remembering Sean's nervous frown as he'd unveiled the custom paint job. We'd all stared in amazement. *If it's too flashy*, he'd started, trailing off. *I can put it back the way it was if you don't like it.*

I'd loved it. Sean had always been the artist of our group.

That nerdy guy—Lenny—who'd brought my bike into the shop had said it wouldn't start. Harper had said she'd look at it in the morning, before she'd locked up the garage and left with Quinn.

But I knew every inch of this machine. I'd taken it apart and put it back together more times than I could count. If it needed fixing, I could do it.

"What do you say?" I patted the leather seat. "Want me to take a look at what's ailing you?"

I moved to Harper's workbench and flicked on the small lamp she kept there, casting just enough light to work by without illuminating the whole garage. I ran my fingertips across Harper's carefully arranged tools and selected a small wrench, the weight familiar and comforting in my hand.

"Let's see what's going on with you, gorgeous."

Four

Harper

"Morning!" Quinn called from her desk, already working on some paperwork despite the early hour. "Dad made the coffee this morning and it's AHH-mazing."

"Thank God," I muttered, making a beeline for the kitchenette.

I poured myself a generous mug and took a long, satisfying sip. The rich flavor danced across my taste buds, making me moan in appreciation. I closed my eyes in a silent moment of thanks to Frank for splurging on the fancy beans.

"You're here early," the hero in question commented, emerging from his office with his own mug in hand. His sharp eyes studied me over the rim as he took a sip.

I shrugged. "Couldn't sleep. Figured I might as well be productive."

Frank nodded knowingly. "Lenny called three times already this morning to check on his bike."

"Of course he did," I sighed, taking another fortifying gulp of coffee. "I'll get right on it."

I headed toward my workstation, already mentally cataloging the likely culprits for the bike's issues. Vintage bikes could be temperamental. I set my coffee on the bench and bent over to pick up the teddy bear that had fallen to the concrete floor.

"Hey, there, buddy. Did someone knock you over?" I ran my hand over his fur and froze as my eyes moved past him to take in the bike at my station.

The bike's gas tank was open, and several components had clearly been removed, serviced, and replaced. The carburetor looked freshly cleaned, and even the spark plugs had been changed.

What the hell?

"Frank?" I called over my shoulder, setting the bear onto the workbench. "Did you work on the Triumph this morning?"

Frank strolled over, his face impassive. "Nope. Figured I'd leave it to the expert." He gestured to me with his mug. "I can't believe how much you got done last night."

"Quinn and I went to dinner." I carefully picked up the immaculate carburetor.

Frank leaned in for a closer look. "This is really nice work." He ran a finger along the metal edge, wiping away a trace of polish.

"We left right after you did," I insisted, shaking my head.

Frank shrugged, unperturbed. "Must've been elves then." He gave me one of his rare half-smiles. "Better check if it starts."

"But—" I began, then stopped myself. What was I going to say? That some mysterious mechanic had broken into the garage overnight to fix Lenny's bike? That sounded certifiably insane.

I closed my mouth and turned back to the Triumph as Frank wandered off. I went slowly, checking each component as I reassembled the engine over the next hour. When I was done, I stood back and examined my work—or our work. Whoever had been my mysterious assistant, they had left the key in the ignition. Hesitantly, I swung a leg over and settled onto the leather seat.

I turned the key and pressed the starter button, bracing myself for disappointment.

The engine burst into song, settling into a perfect, throaty purr that made goosebumps rise on my arms. The sound was mechanical perfection—balanced, powerful, and smooth as silk.

Frank appeared at my side as if summoned by the magic of the engine's song and nodded appreciatively, his expression soft. "You do good work, Harper."

I turned to face my boss directly. "Frank, I swear I didn't touch this bike last night. Someone else must have been in here."

Frank's eyes narrowed slightly. "The alarm was set when I opened up this morning. No one else was in here except for the three of us. And you know we don't let Quinn touch anything mechanical since the incident."

"I heard that!" came an accusatory cry from Quinn's desk. "I thought we weren't going to bring that up anymore."

I shook my head at Frank. "Then how—"

"You don't have to be modest," he interrupted, patting me awkwardly on the shoulder. "It's okay to take credit for good work."

Before I could protest further, Quinn bounced over. "Holy crap, that sounds amazing!" she exclaimed, her eyes wide. "You're like the bike whisperer or something!"

I gave up, killing the engine and dismounting as Frank drifted back into his office. "Yeah, I guess so." I ran a hand through my hair, bewildered. "Could you call Lenny and tell him his bike's ready?" I asked Quinn.

As she skipped off to make the call, I surveyed my workstation more carefully. I wasn't just being paranoid—something was definitely off. Someone had been here in my space, moving around my tools. Everything had been put back in its place, but it wasn't quite perfect. I knew that would sound crazy if I said it out loud, but I could tell.

My gaze landed on a piece of fabric pooled on the concrete floor in front of my workbench. I crouched down and picked it up—one of the garage's spare coveralls. They were stained with grease and oil, clearly recently used.

I lifted them to eye level, examining the stains. As I brought them closer, the hint of a spicy scent wafted toward me and I buried my nose in the fabric without thought.

The scent that filled my nostrils made my knees go weak. Motor oil and metal, yes, but underneath that was leather and something that reminded me of stormy nights. It was familiar. I breathed in again, searching my brain. Where had I smelled this exact combination of...

Man?

Oh, my god. The naked man from my dream.

I dropped the coveralls like they'd burned me, my heart pounding in my ears. This was ridiculous. I was definitely losing it. They probably just smelled like that because Frank had been wearing them, or maybe one of the customers had borrowed them.

But I was pretty sure Frank didn't smell like that. And we hadn't had any customers in the garage area recently.

I scooped the coveralls off the concrete floor and shoved them into the laundry bin with more force than necessary and turned back to the Triumph, determined to get a grip on myself. This was just stress, lack of sleep, and an overactive imagination. Time to get back to work.

The morning dragged by as I helped other customers, all while keeping one eye on the clock. Lenny had said he'd be by "after lunch," which could mean anything from 1:00 PM to closing time. Finally, a little after two, Lenny burst through the front door, practically bouncing with excitement.

"Quinn said she's ready? Please tell me she's ready!" he begged, adjusting his glasses. His t-shirt featured the silhouettes of various famous spaceships from popular fiction.

"All set," I confirmed, gesturing toward the bike. "Give her a try."

Lenny rushed over to the Triumph, his hands fluttering over it without quite touching, as if it was too precious for direct contact. "What was wrong with her?"

I hesitated, not sure what to say since I hadn't actually been the one to fix it. "Carburetor needed cleaning," I finally offered, figuring that was a safe bet based on what I'd seen. "And new spark plugs. Nothing major."

"You're a miracle worker!" Lenny gushed. "Do you know what this means? The last link to the Santa Paola

Six will be front and center at the convention this weekend!"

"Right," I said. "That's the gang that disappeared?"

Lenny's eyes lit up so brightly I immediately regretted asking.

"They weren't really a gang-gang. They were more like a club. It was Labor Day weekend, 1975," he began, lowering his voice dramatically. "Six young men, all in their twenties. They weren't into anything illegal—but they had the look. Leather jackets, cool bikes, that whole James Dean vibe."

He gestured to the Triumph. "This beauty belonged to their leader, Ronan O'Neill."

I froze at the name and the room spun around me. "Ronan?" I repeated weakly.

"Yeah, he had a garage right on the edge of town." Lenny pushed his glasses up his nose. "Anyway, that night they all met at the boardwalk. Witnesses claimed there were raised voices and bright lights."

He paused for dramatic effect. "And then, poof! They vanished."

"What do you mean, vanished?" I croaked.

"I mean, one minute they were there on the pier, and the next they were gone. All that was left were their bikes, parked in a perfect row." He pointed to the Triumph. "This baby sat unclaimed for weeks before the police finally impounded the bikes as evidence."

I couldn't stop my gaze from flashing to the bear on my workbench, to the little name tag on his ear. Coincidence. It had to be.

"Evidence of what?" I asked, trying to keep my voice steady.

"That's the million-dollar question!" Lenny exclaimed. "Some say they were abducted by aliens or made some kind of deal with the devil. Some say they were targeted by the mob after an arson attempt gone wrong. There's even a theory that they stumbled onto a government experiment and were 'disappeared.'" He made air quotes around the last word.

"Or maybe they just went for a swim and drowned," I suggested pragmatically.

Lenny shook his head vigorously. "Nope. No bodies ever washed up. And the coast guard searched for days."

"So what do you think happened to them?" I asked, genuinely curious despite my skepticism.

Lenny leaned in close, his voice dropping to a whisper. "I think they're still here. Trapped somehow. Watching and waiting."

A shiver ran down my spine, and I had to force out a laugh. "That's...quite a theory." I stepped back, needing some space. "Well, your bike is all set. Quinn has your paperwork."

A few minutes later Lenny rode off on his perfectly tuned Triumph, but I couldn't shake the strange feeling that had settled over me. My gaze was drawn back over to my workbench, where Ronan the bear sat, his green glass eyes reflecting the overhead lights.

Just a really weird coincidence.

That night, I made sure to bring the bear home with me.

"Not making that mistake again," I told him as I placed him back on my nightstand. "I barely slept last night without you. How pathetic is that?"

The teddy bear stared back at me with its unchanging expression.

I went through my evening routine, trying to ignore the toy's watchful gaze as I brushed my teeth, washed my face, and changed into an oversized t-shirt. Finally, I crawled into bed, turning off the lamp and snuggling under the covers.

After a few minutes of lying in the darkness, I reached out and pulled the bear into my arms.

"This is stupid," I whispered into his fur. "I'm a grown woman cuddling a teddy bear."

Yet there was something deeply comforting about holding him close, feeling his weight against my chest. He smelled faintly of motor oil and metal, like the garage. And just faintly, under that, was an earthier sm ell...

I drifted into sleep, wrapped in the scent of leather and rain.

Ronan

I held perfectly still, taking in the familiar surroundings—Harper's room, Harper's bed. *Harper.*

Her body was molded to mine. Her slow, steady breaths warmed my chest, each exhale a gentle caress against my skin. I lifted my hand—my human hand—and marveled at the freedom of movement. My fingers hovered over her hair for a moment before gently tracing the silken strands.

"So soft," I whispered, barely louder than a breath.

In sleep, her face lost the subtle tension it carried all day. Those slight furrows between her brows that appeared whenever Quinn's dad gave her a particularly challenging job, or when she was concentrating on a tricky repair—they were all smoothed away now.

Her eyelashes fluttered against her cheeks, and I froze. But she only sighed and nestled closer, her arm tightening around my waist.

God, the sweet torture of her body pressed against mine. Being trapped in that damn claw machine for fifty years had been hell. But this? This was a different kind of torture altogether.

And I loved it.

"What are you doing to me?" I murmured into her hair.

Carefully, I disentangled myself from her embrace, sliding out from under the covers. Cold air hit my naked skin, raising goosebumps across my arms and chest.

Harper made a small sound of protest, reaching for the empty space I'd left behind. I tucked the covers around her, and she settled again, burying her face into my pillow.

I padded across the worn wooden floor, wincing at a particularly loud creak. Harper didn't stir. The faint silver moonlight streaming through the thin curtains cast everything in ghostly relief.

The bedroom was small but neat, with mismatched furniture that worked together to create a casual, cozy warmth. A battered dresser in one corner, a small desk with one of those laptop computer things in another. Above the desk hung a framed diploma. I squinted at it in the dim light.

"Harper Brinkman, Bachelor of Science in Mechanical Engineering," I read in a hushed voice. "Wow."

Smart as hell, this one. Not just a grease monkey, but an engineer. I knew the world had changed in the last fifty years—but that was still an accomplishment.

Moving to the dresser, I cautiously opened a drawer. Neat stacks of t-shirts and jeans, practical and no-nonsense, just like their owner. A faint scent of lavender rose from the clothes, the same clean, fresh scent that clung to her hair and reminded me of the sachets my mom used to keep in her dresser.

I carefully avoided looking in the mirror that hung above the dresser and continued my exploration, moving silently into the hallway. The cottage was tiny—a small bathroom across from the bedroom, and a combined living room and kitchen at the end of the short hall. Everything was modestly furnished but tidy.

In the kitchen, I marveled at the appliances. The refrigerator hummed quietly, a sleek silver monster twice the size of the ones I remembered. I opened it, the light inside momentarily blinding me. Half-empty takeout containers, condiments, a lonely six-pack of beer. The food of someone who lived alone and didn't cook much.

"Typical bachelor refrigerator," I chuckled. Some things didn't change.

I closed the door and moved to the living room. A small couch faced a flat black screen mounted on the wall. No cabinet, no knobs or dials, just a thin black rectangle.

"What the hell?" I muttered, approaching it cautiously. If this was a television, it had evolved far beyond the chunky boxes I remembered. There were no antennas in sight.

A small bookshelf stood in the corner, filled with an eclectic mix of paperbacks and hardcovers. I ran my fingers along the spines—service manuals for various cars and motorcycles, a few sci-fi novels, and surprisingly, a collection of classic poetry.

A bubble of happiness escaped me as a sigh. A stunningly beautiful grease monkey who reads poetry? No wonder I had to wait fifty years.

Harper was definitely one in a million.

A small table by the sofa held a framed photograph—a younger Harper with an older man standing proudly beside a battered old Volkswagen. Both were covered in grease and grinning like idiots. The resemblance was unmistakable.

"It must run in the family," I said to the photo, tapping the glass lightly.

A small rectangular device on the coffee table lit up suddenly, vibrating against the wood. I approached it warily. I'd seen people using these wireless phones at the boardwalk for years.

The screen displayed a message labeled with Quinn's name.

RU UP?

I frowned at the device. How did it work? I tapped the screen experimentally and jumped when the words rolled up. I ran my finger over the text and it flowed up, revealing a series of short messages between Harper and Quinn.

I read their exchanges with fascination. Most were casual—discussions about work, plans for dinner, Quinn's relentless attempts to get Harper to go out more often.

And then a name jumped out: *Douchebag Derek.*

Martha ran into Douchebag Derek at the grocery store. She said he's been asking about you. I told her to tell him to go to hell.

Harper's reply sent a chill through my veins.

Please god don't let him find out where I am.

I set the phone down, frowning. I hated that Harper was afraid of her ex. I'd been listening to her and Quinn's conversations and I recognized the type—bullies who mistook control for love, who thought a woman was a possession rather than a partner.

Moving back to the bedroom doorway, I watched Harper sleeping peacefully. She'd traveled across states to escape this Derek. Built a new life. Found safety in this little coastal town.

"You don't have to be afraid of Derek or anyone else," I promised her sleeping form. "Not while I have breath in my body."

I moved to stand in front of Harper's dresser again and this time I let my gaze take in a face I hadn't seen for fifty years. It was the same square shape, the same wavy hair flopping over the high forehead to just graze the top of thick brows. There were no new wrinkles around the eyes, no gray in the black hair. I ran my hand over the tattoo that wrapped around my upper arm. How had it been fifty years?

Magic.

The irony of my statement to Harper wasn't lost on me—I had only been human for a few hours and I had no way to predict or control the next change. What protection could I really offer her while I was at the mercy of this curse?

Five

Harper

Quinn was at her desk, her fingers flying across her keyboard, when I stumbled in the next morning. She looked up, her eyes widening as she took in my disheveled appearance.

"Holy bedhead, Batman," she said, abandoning her typing to stare at me. "Did you stick your finger in an electrical socket?"

"Good morning to you too," I muttered, making a beeline for the coffee pot. "Is Frank here yet?"

"Been and gone. Supply run." She abandoned her desk and followed me to the kitchenette. "I texted you like fifty times last night. Where were you?"

I poured myself a cup of coffee and took a life-giving sip. "Sleeping like an absolute rock, apparently. I don't think I've slept that well in years."

"You didn't read any of my messages?" Quinn asked with a frown, bouncing on her toes.

"No." I took another sip of coffee, closing my eyes as the caffeine seeped into my tired veins. "Normal people don't answer the phone after midnight, you know. Also, I left my phone in the living room—"

Quinn grabbed my shoulders, cutting me off and nearly making me spill my coffee.

"Hey!" I protested.

"Derek called me last night," Quinn announced, her gaze searching my face.

The mug began to slip from my suddenly numb fingers and Quinn released her death grip on me to rescue it. She set it back on the counter while I learned how to breathe again.

"What did he say?" My voice was a raspy whisper.

Quinn grabbed paper towels and knelt to mop up the droplets of coffee that had ended up on the floor. "He was all like, 'Hey, Quinn,'" she mimicked in a deep, obnoxious voice as she wiped the floor aggressively. "Like we were old friends or something. He wanted to know if I'd talked to you lately."

My heart hammered against my ribs. "What did you tell him?"

"That I hadn't seen you for months and I heard you moved to Seattle with your lesbian lover in a U-Haul full of motorcycle parts and cats." Quinn stood up, wadding the soaked paper towels into a ball.

Despite the fear curling in my stomach, a small laugh escaped. "Thanks."

"He sounded weird, though." Quinn tossed the paper towels in the trash and put her hands on her hips. "Like, extra douchebag-y. Very polite and very angry."

"Did he say anything else?"

"Just that if I happened to run into you, I should tell you to get in touch." She squeezed my arm. "Harp, do you think he knows you're here?"

The garage door burst open. Quinn and I both spun around, but it was just Frank, carrying two paper bags of supplies.

"Morning," he called gruffly, shouldering the door closed and shuffling past us to the store room without a glance.

"I'll be fine," I whispered to Quinn. "He was probably just calling all of my old friends. It doesn't mean anything."

We both ignored the tremor in my hands as I picked up my mug from the counter.

I found solace in the steady, logical problems of broken machines. Cars made sense. They had diagrams, manuals, and logic. Unlike people, who could smile at you one moment and slam their fist into your face the next.

I was halfway under a Subaru when a pair of men's loafers appeared in my peripheral vision.

"Harper?"

Scrambling out from under the car, I banged my head on the chassis. Stars exploded behind my eyes as pain radiated through my skull.

"Are you alright?" Lenny's face swam into view.

Not Derek.

"I'm so sorry! I didn't mean to startle you." Lenny dropped to his knees at my side, flapping his hands around me ineffectually.

"It's okay." I focused on slowing my breathing as I pressed my palm against the throbbing spot on my forehead. "That was one hundred percent my own fault."

"Can I get you some ice?" Lenny asked, looking like he was in more pain than I was. "I'm really sorry."

"Nope, I'm okay." I accepted Lenny's hand to get to my feet, still keeping pressure on my head. I was going to have a lovely bump. "What can I do for you, Lenny?"

He pulled an envelope from his pocket and offered it to me with a sheepish smile. "I just wanted to offer you two VIP passes to SPConCon this weekend. As a thank you for getting the Triumph running again so quickly." He shook his head in amazement, his smile relaxing into a wide grin. "It sounds better than it has in years. You're a miracle worker, Harper."

I accepted the envelope as graciously as possible. "Oh, that really isn't necessary, Lenny. But thank you. I'm just happy your bike is running again."

"You know, I don't really think of it as my bike." He leaned in, lowering his voice. "Ronan O'Neill was quite the mechanical genius. Some say he could diagnose an engine problem just by listening to it run."

"Is that so?"

"Indeed. His personal tools are part of our exhibition. They're not that different than what you have here, really." He straightened up. "I hope you'll consider attending. I know you're new to town—it's a wonderful way to connect with local history."

"I'll think about it," I promised, knowing full well I wouldn't go.

Lenny nodded, apparently satisfied. "Excellent. I look forward to seeing you there."

As he walked away, Quinn materialized at my side. "What was that about?"

I waved the envelope. "Apparently I've been cordially invited to Nerd-Con."

"Ooh, fun! We should totally go!" She snatched the envelope from my hands. "I've never been, but I hear they have some seriously spooky exhibits. Ghost hunting equipment, grainy photos of supposed alien spacecraft—"

"Hard pass." I grabbed my fallen wrench and slid back under the car, seeking refuge in its familiar metal parts.

My tiny little rental cottage had never looked more inviting as I pushed through the door that evening. After a day of jumping at every sound, I was mentally and physically exhausted.

After changing out of my work clothes, I made myself dinner and tried to relax, collapsing onto my couch with a generous glass of wine. The house was quiet except for the gentle ticking of the clock and the distant rhythm of waves crashing on the shore.

"Get it together, Harper," I muttered to myself, taking a long swallow of wine and letting my head fall back. "Jumping at shadows isn't going to help anything."

I was half asleep when my phone rang, shattering the silence. Quinn's name flashed on the screen.

"Hey," I answered. "Is everything okay?"

"He's here." Quinn's voice was tight with panic. "Derek is here in Santa Paola."

The room tilted sideways. "How do you know?" My voice sounded far away, like it belonged to someone else.

"My cousin Lisa works at the Beachside Inn. She was telling me about this hot white guy who came in for dinner and how weird it was that he was asking about local mechanic shops." Quinn's words came in a frantic rush. "I asked her if she remembered his name and she didn't, but it has to be him."

I wanted to argue, but my voice was stuck in my throat.

"Harp, there aren't that many repair shops in town. It's just a matter of time."

A loud crash from the back of the house made me jump to my feet, wine glass tumbling to the floor, forgotten.

"What was that?" Quinn asked.

"I don't know. Hold on." My biggest wrench was still under my pillow in the bedroom, so I grabbed the frying pan sitting on top of the stove and crept down the hallway.

Quinn was starting to panic over the phone, her voice rising. "Harper?"

"Shhh," I tried to hush her, moving the phone away from my ear and raising the hand with the frying pan.

The door to my room was ajar, a sliver of light visible through the crack. My heart hammered in my throat as I nudged it open with my foot.

A naked man sat on the floor in front of my nightstand.

A gorgeous, familiar naked man with tousled black hair and piercing green eyes that locked with mine the instant I stepped into the doorway.

Not Derek.

But still—naked. *Focus, Harper!*

"Harper," he said, his voice a rich, deep rumble that sent goose bumps racing across my skin. "Are you okay?"

"Am *I* okay?" I waved the frying pan in a threatening manner, keeping my eyes firmly north of the border. "Who the hell are you and why are you in my house?"

And my dreams?

"I'm Ronan." He held up his hands, pulling my gaze back down. "And I think I'm here because you're my soulmate."

"Soulmate?" I repeated dumbly, the frying pan lowering as I took in swathes of golden skin. He was so very naked. *Eyes up, Harper!* My phone was screeching, the sounds faint and tinny, but I ignored it. "What are you talking about?"

He gestured behind him to the nightstand. "I was sitting there."

"You were sitting on my nightstand?" I asked dubiously.

The naked man had no such reservations. "I was a bear," he said as if that were a completely sane statement.

"A bear?" My gaze moved to the empty nightstand behind him. Ronan the teddy bear wasn't sitting where I left him. "Where's Ronan?" I asked, frying pan coming back up. "What did you do with my teddy bear, you pervert?"

"I'm Ronan," he repeated, draping his hands strategically across his lap.

I dragged my eyes back up to meet his. "You're Ronan?" Hysteria bubbled up from my chest. "You're telling me you're my teddy bear?"

"I know it sounds crazy," he said, his face deadly serious. "But it's true. I'm Ronan O'Neill and I've been stuck under a curse since 1975."

A laugh burst out of me against my will. Yup, that sounded crazy all right. "You're seriously trying to tell me you're a teddy bear?"

"I'm human, I swear." He ran a hand through his hair, looking frustrated. "Or I was. I'm not sure exactly what I am now."

"Like a werewolf," I said, then immediately wanted to smack myself. It was insane to entertain this. I was standing in my bedroom having a conversation with a naked lunatic.

And yet...

"I dreamed about you," I said slowly, "the night I won the teddy bear from the claw machine."

His eyes softened. "It wasn't a dream, Harper."

"And at the garage?" My mind was racing now. "The coveralls that smelled like you. You fixed the Triumph?"

He nodded. "That's my bike. Or it was."

"In 1975," I finished for him, my voice barely above a whisper. "So you're telling me you've been trapped as a teddy bear for fifty years?"

"In that damn claw machine on the boardwalk," he confirmed. "Until you saved me."

"And now you're human again...sometimes?"

"I think it's you—" He stopped abruptly.

The door behind me flew the rest of the way open and Quinn appeared like an avenging angel in a footed unicorn onesie.

"I BROUGHT A BASEBALL BAT AND I'M NOT AFRAID TO USE IT!" she yelled, raising said bat over her head.

"Jesus, Quinn!" I gasped. "Were you planning to take on the entire neighborhood?"

She lowered the baseball bat, her eyes wild as she searched my bedroom. "Are you okay? Where's Derek?"

"He isn't here. This is—" I turned, the hand with the frying pan raising to gesture toward the spot where a naked man had just been sitting on my carpet.

There was only a teddy bear.

I walked over to the bed, throwing the frying pan and the phone onto it, and picked up the bear. He was heavy, and warm.

"No one's here." The lie fell easily from my lips. "I was half asleep and the bear fell off the nightstand. Made a huge crash. I think I was having a weird dream when you called."

Quinn peered suspiciously over my shoulder, then back at me. "You're sure? Because I swear I heard a man's voice."

"Just talking to myself." I smiled weakly.

She studied me for a long moment, then her eyes dropped to the bear in my arms. "Since when do you sleep with stuffed animals?"

I walked past her, toward the living room. "Want some wine? I think we could both use a drink."

Quinn hesitated, then nodded, propping her baseball bat against the wall. "Fine. But if there's a naked man hiding in your closet, I reserve the right to say I told you so before beating him senseless."

"Deal." I turned toward the kitchen, still clutching Ronan tightly in my arms.

Six

"I deserve this," I groaned into my pillow as my alarm blared its obnoxious electronic trill. I'd spent half the night sitting on the couch drinking wine with Quinn, reassuring her—and myself—that everything was fine while desperately clutching a teddy bear like a security blanket.

Ronan, the teddy bear who was also sometimes a hot naked guy.

I think. Or maybe that had been a wine-induced dream brought on by stress and Lenny's conspiracy theories. I pulled my head out from under the blankets and blinked at the sunlight streaming through my thin curtains.

The nightstand was empty.

Had I left the bear in the living room, with Quinn passed out on my couch. An unreasonable spark of something that might have been jealousy zipped up my spine. I pushed myself up in the bed and the smell of bacon slammed into my nose like a freight train.

My brain glitched as I tried to process the sensory information. I'd lived with Quinn for four years through college and there was no way she was making me breakfast. For one thing, the fire alarm wasn't going off.

Grabbing the wrench from under my pillow, I moved toward my bedroom door on silent feet and slipped into the hallway. My pulse pounded in my ears, nearly drowning out the quiet clink of dishes coming from the kitchen.

Deep breaths, Harper.

Brandishing my wrench like the world's dorkiest ninja, I peered around the corner.

A shirtless man stood at my stove, wearing nothing but a pair of gray sweatpants that were about three sizes too small and six inches too short. A black tattoo wound around his upper arm.

Not Derek.

"Ronan?" My voice squeaked out embarrassingly high.

He spun around, spatula raised like a weapon. "Jesus, Harper. You scared me."

"*I* scared *you*?" I gestured broadly with my wrench. "What are you doing?"

"Making breakfast," he stated calmly, turning back to the stove. "I found eggs and bacon in your fridge. There's coffee too."

The rich aroma of coffee hit my nose, making my mouth water. "No. No breakfast. No coffee. I need answers." I put my hand on my hip. "Now."

"Now what?" Quinn's head popped up from behind the couch, her unicorn hoodie pulled low over her forehead, limp horn hanging down sadly past her bleary, hung over eyes.

The spatula clattered onto the kitchen floor, beside a pair of gray sweatpants and an innocent looking teddy bear.

Five hours later Quinn was looking somewhat more professional in a pair of khakis and a polo with the garage's name embroidered over the pocket. The fact that she was sitting with her head lying on her desk kind of ruined the image, though.

Placing the socket I'd been using back in its cradle, I wandered over to make sure she was still breathing.

"Quinn?" I said gently, placing a hand on her shoulder.

Her head popped up, eyes still closed. "I'm awake," she blurted out, then laid her head back on the desk. "I'm completely awake."

I just shook my head. "It's a good thing your dad isn't here today," I told her.

Her head shot back up, this time her eyes narrowed as she frowned at me suspiciously. "Why are you awake?" she asked accusingly. "You had just as much wine as I did."

"I've got like six inches and thirty pounds on you," I pointed out reasonably.

She flapped her hand at me, pushing back from the desk and getting to her feet with a sigh. "Yeah, yeah," she dismissed my logical argument. "Speaking of pounds, I'm going to walk down to the diner and get some lunch. Maybe that will wake me up." Quinn pulled her bag from the bottom drawer of the desk and tugged it into place over her shoulder. "Can I bring you back something?"

I dug a five out of my pocket and passed it over. "A turkey sandwich and fries would be great. I'll hold down the fort."

Quinn hustled out the door, appearing much more alert with the prospect of food on the horizon, and I went back to the radiator I was working on. Leaning over the front end of the ford, I was elbow deep in grease trying to loosen a stubborn bolt when I dropped my ratchet. It tumbled through the engine and clanged against the concrete floor while I cursed a blue streak.

"Try this one," a smooth deep voice suggested as a slightly smaller caliber tool appeared at my shoulder.

I froze. "Ronan?"

"Don't turn around," he said quickly.

"Why not?" I whispered.

There was a long pause, the heat of his body searing along my back.

"I'm naked," he finally admitted sheepishly.

My eyes widened but I kept my gaze focused on the cold metal in front of me. "Oh."

"Oh, indeed," he chuckled. "Try this rachet, though." He wiggled the tool in the periphery of my vision. "I think it will do the job for you."

Tentatively, I took the tool. It was heavy in my hand as I used it to loosen the bolt, which released with a sigh. I worked it loose until the entire casing came away, revealing the issue.

"Thanks," I said softly.

"Anytime." There was a smile in Ronan's voice. "I used to be pretty good at this stuff." He shifted his weight and his breath stirred the hairs at the nape of my neck.

Focus, Harper.

"Before you were a bear," I managed.

"Exactly." His hand brushed mine as he took back the tool.

Metal clattered against concrete and I spun around, but he was gone. The teddy bear lay askew on the floor beside the abandoned tool.

"Harper!" Quinn burst into the garage like a redhead-ed tornado. "Oh my god, Harper!"

My heart plummeted. "What's wrong?"

"I just saw him." Quinn's face was ghost-white. "Derek. He was walking down Main Street like he owned the place."

I bent to pick up Ronan and the ratchet, buying time to slow my racing pulse.

"Did he see you?" I asked, straightening up.

"No, I don't think so." Quinn faced hardened, the color returning to her face. "We're going to go talk to Chief Hudson."

I pressed my lips together to silence my protests as Quinn locked up the garage and frog-marched me down main street to the Santa Paola PD. The station blend-ed in with the other charming storefronts, with a large glass window featuring ornate gold lettering. Despite the quaint exterior, the inside was sleek and modern with an open layout. A long counter separated the lobby area from the bullpen. A uniformed officer with a bouncy blonde ponytail hopped up from her desk when we walked in.

"Hey, Quinnie!" she chirped. "Set off any fire alarms lately?"

Quinn waved the comment away. "It's been ten years, Meredith. Get over it. We need to see your dad."

"You know the way." She leaned over to hold open the swinging gate with a smile that stretched from ear to ear. As Quinn shuffled past her, Meredith stage-whispered, "Juvenile delinquent."

"Nepo baby," Quinn replied, without missing a beat.

My eyes were huge as Quinn glanced back at me as we moved down the hall.

"We went to high school together," she shrugged, dismissively.

In the last office at the end of the hall, we found Chief Hudson sitting at a big modern desk holding three huge monitors.

The Santa Paola Chief of Police was a mountain of a man. He listened intently as Quinn ranted about Derek's verbal abuse and controlling behavior, reaching into his desk to pull out a bottle of chewable antacids.

"So this Derek fellow," Chief Hudson said once Quinn wound down, "he's your ex-boyfriend?" He directed the question at me, popping an antacid into his mouth and leaning back in his chair until it creaked in protest.

"Yes, sir." My fingers itched to hold onto something—preferably my wrench or Ronan—but I'd left both at the garage.

"And he hit you?" The chief's voice was gentler now.

"Yes." The word came out barely above a whisper. I forced myself to meet his eyes. "Just once."

Chief Hudson's weathered face creased as he frowned. "Once is enough. Did you file a report?"

"No." My chest burned. "I just left."

"Smart girl." The chief popped another antacid.

Quinn leaned forward in her chair. "But now he's here, Chief. He's looking for her."

"Has he actually approached either of you?" he asked. "Made any direct contact?"

"Well, no," Quinn admitted. "But he called me. And I saw him on Main Street today."

Chief Hudson sighed heavily, parking his elbows on his desk and rubbing his temples. "Listen, girls. I take this kind of thing very seriously. But with this convention starting tomorrow, the department is stretched thin with all the extra visitors in town."

"So you're not going to do anything?" Quinn demanded, her voice rising.

"I didn't say that." The chief held up a calming hand. "I'll put out an alert to my officers to keep an eye out for this Derek character. What's his last name?"

"Dufort," I supplied. "Derek Dufort."

Chief Hudson scribbled the name on a notepad. "Address? Do you have a photo?"

I rattled off Derek's address and pulled out my phone and found an old picture of us at a college football game in happier times. Derek stood tall and blond behind me, his hair perfectly swept off of his forehead and his arm wrapped around my shoulder. I had just come from work and sported a wrinkled shirt and a messy ponytail.

I handed the phone to the chief.

He studied the image. "Good looking kid," he commented. "They usually are." He passed the phone back and handed me a business card. "Send that to this email address. Where are you staying?"

"I'm renting the little blue cottage at the end of Ocean View Drive."

"Alone?"

I nodded.

He plucked the card I was still holding from my hand and wrote something on the back. "Here, this is my personal cell. You see this asshole anywhere near you, you call me immediately. Day or night."

I accepted the card, touched by his gruff concern. "Thank you."

"One more thing." The chief's pale blue eyes locked onto mine. "Stop over at the hardware store and get yourself a can of pepper spray. Tell Dan I sent you, he'll give you the good stuff."

"Yes, sir."

He stood up, signaling the end of our meeting. "Now if you'll excuse me, I need to go deal with the dozen complaints we've already received today about conspiracy theorists trespassing on private property. This damn convention gives me an ulcer every year." He shook his head.

As we walked out of the station Quinn ignored Meredith and looped her arm through mine. "See? That wasn't so bad."

"I guess not." The weight of the chief's card was reassuring in my pocket.

As we walked down Main Street, I found myself scanning every face we passed, tension coiling in my shoulders. Would Derek be openly walking around town? Or would he be lurking in shadows, watching, waiting for the right moment?

"Stop that," Quinn commanded.

"Stop what?"

"Looking like you expect him to jump out from behind every building." She tugged me toward the hardware store. "You're not alone, Harper. You've got me, and dad, and Chief Hudson. I bet even Mrs. Peterson would throw a punch for you."

The bell above the hardware store door chimed as we entered. Dan, the owner, looked up from his newspaper.

"Good afternoon," he called out cheerfully. "What can I do for you ladies today?"

Quinn marched right up to the counter. "Chief Hudson sent us. We need your strongest pepper spray."

Dan's jovial expression turned serious. "Did he now?" His eyes moved between us. "Say no more, ladies."

He disappeared into the back room and returned with a small black canister. "This is the good stuff. Military grade." He demonstrated how to remove the safety and properly aim it. "But be careful. The spray pattern is wide, so make sure you're upwind."

I reached for my wallet but Dan waved me off. "On the house. Chief Hudson wouldn't have sent you if you didn't need it."

"Thank you," I said quietly, tucking the pepper spray into my pocket beside the chief's card.

"You need anything else?" Dan asked. "Baseball bat? Door locks? Security cameras?"

Quinn's eyes lit up. "Actually..."

Seven

The screw for the new strike plate slid into the hole I'd pre-drilled and settled into the bevel so that the head sat flush with the shiny brass surface. I pushed back onto my heels to admire the perfect fit as a thump sounded from the couch behind me.

"There are pants on the coffee table," I announced without looking back.

Ronan choked out a laugh. "You're prepared," he said as the sounds of rustling cloth came from mere feet behind me.

I tried not to picture him pulling the largest pair of sweatpants I owned over his bare legs..and other parts. I failed.

Down, girl.

"Yup. My troop leader would be proud." I tucked my screwdriver back into its kit. "I'm prepared for unexpected rainstorms, stalker ex-boyfriends, and magical teddy bears that turn into naked men."

It got quiet behind me. "These are a little short."

"Beggars can't be choosers, buddy." I closed the front door, doing a final test of the alignment of the new security bolt. "Though we should probably get you some clothes if you're going to be sticking around."

"Do you want that?" His voice held a note of hope that made my heart do a funny little flip.

"Well, yeah." I finally turned around to face him. The sweatpants hung low on his hips and ended several inches above his ankles. His upper body was bare, revealing an expanse of tanned skin and the tattoo that wrapped around his bicep. "Unless you'd rather be back in that claw machine?"

"God, no." He ran a hand through his disheveled dark hair. "Though I did learn a lot watching the world go by. It's nice to be able to put that knowledge to the test now."

"So you can see and hear when you're a bear?"

He nodded and stepped close, reaching for my hand. "Which is often torture. I could see how upset you were today and I couldn't do anything about it." His fingers, rough and warm, squeezed mine. "I just want to protect you."

"I'm okay." I gave him a lopsided smile. "I've got pepper spray."

Ronan's expression stayed serious. "I'm not sure that will do much."

"Hence the new deadbolt." I pulled my hand away gently and began cleaning up my tools. "Quinn made me get a motion light for the front porch, too."

"Good idea."

Tools in hand, I turned back to face Ronan. "She's a really good friend."

Ronan searched my face. "You should have let her stay with you. I know she offered."

"But then I wouldn't—" I cut myself off, biting my lip.

"You wouldn't what?"

Ronan suddenly seemed so much closer. It took a lot of effort not to drop gaze from his.

I let out a shaky breath. "I figured if Quinn stayed, I wouldn't get to see you."

"This is amazing," Ronan gushed, shoving another spoonful of cream golden noodles between his full lips.

Warmth flooded my cheeks and I hid behind my glass of milk for a moment as I took a sip. "Thanks. I pretty much survived on mac and cheese throughout college."

Ronan swallowed his bite. "You studied engineering? Most mechanics go to trade school."

"Yeah." I blew on my cheesy noodles. "My dad really wanted me to get my degree." I chewed my food, flooded with memories.

"He must have been so proud of you," Ronan said softly.

I nodded. Sadness still rushed into my chest, but time had dulled the pain. "He passed away during my junior year, but I know he was." I sat my spoon down and blotted at my lips with my napkin. "My mom passed away when I was little. She was a college professor and my dad kind of felt like me being a mechanic like him wasn't fair. He wanted me to get my degree because he knew it would have been important to her."

"That makes sense." Ronan reached out to place his hand over mine and give it a gentle squeeze, the weight solid and warm. "But you're not using your degree?" He probed gently.

"I was." I took a shaky breath. "Derek encouraged me to take a job as an automotive engineer after graduation. It was a good opportunity, according to him."

"You didn't like it?" He guessed, reading between the lines.

I choked out a laugh. "I hated it. How did you know?"

Ronan smiled, sliding his hand away to scoop up the last bite of his mac and cheese. "I can tell you like being elbow deep inside an engine, getting your hands dirty."

"Yup," I agreed, standing to grab both of our empty bowls. "And Derek *hated* that. Everytime I came home with grease under my nails he had an unholy fit. We fought about it all the time."

Ronan came to stand beside me at the sink. As I finished washing a plate he took it gently from me and dried it. His large, calloused hands, with the familiar scars of a mechanic over the knuckles, moved my pretty pink dish towel over each plate with care and precision before placing it back on the shelf above us.

I handed him the last dish and he caught my gaze.

"It was his loss," Ronan said firmly. "He knows that now and that's why he wants you back."

My lips firmed. "Well, he can't have me." I turned away to wipe down the sink. "The breakup was hard, but I'm so much happier now. Here in this crazy little town, working in Frank's garage."

Ronan bumped my shoulder gently with his. "Starting over is always hard."

I sighed and turned to face him. "My dad always said, sometimes you have to break things to fix them."

"Speaking of fixing things..." Ronan peered through the window above the sink at the small garage behind my cottage. "Do you have a car hiding in there?"

"Kind of." Heat crept up my neck. "It's a personal project."

"Can I see it?"

I hesitated and Ronan squinted at me.

"More personal than me showing up naked in your house every night?"

I snorted. "When you put it that way..." Without thinking, I grabbed his hand and pulled him to the door. "Come on."

The evening air was crisp as we crossed the small yard. Dead leaves crunched under our feet and the distant crash of waves provided a familiar backbeat.

I walked past the big garage door and led Ronan to the small side entrance. I had to let go of his hand to unlock the door. Inside, I flicked on the single bare bulb that hung from the ceiling. Dust motes danced in the yellow light.

"This is Junebug," I said softly. "She was my dad's."

The vintage VW Beetle sat in the center of the small space, her faded yellow paint telling the story of decades in the sun. The engine was mostly disassembled, parts organized meticulously on a nearby workbench.

"She's beautiful." Ronan moved closer, running his hand reverently over her rounded fender.

"My dad bought her when I was twelve." The words tumbled out. "Said every father-daughter duo needed a project car. When he died and I had to sell the house, I put her into storage."

I picked up a wrench, weighing the familiar metal in my palm. "The first thing I did when I moved into this house was rescue Junebug and bring her here. Dad loved engines and he was determined to teach me everything he knew about fixing them."

"He did a good job."

"Yeah." I smiled at the memory. "And I really loved it, right from the beginning." The wrench turned over and over in my hands. "Then I met Derek. He said working in a garage was beneath me. That I should be designing cars, not fixing them."

"Asshole," Ronan muttered.

"Total asshole," I agreed. "But I believed him. Took a fancy job in an office, sitting at a computer all day." I grimaced at the new grease under my fingernails. "My hands stayed clean but I was miserable."

Ronan reached out and caught my hand, bringing it to his lips. The kiss he pressed to my knuckles sent electricity zinging up my arm.

"These hands," he said, his voice rough, "are perfect exactly as they are."

Then his mouth was on mine and my brain short-circuited.

His lips were soft but insistent, one hand tangling in my hair while the other pulled me closer. He tasted familiar, like summer storms and possibilities. My fingers splayed across his bare chest, his heart thundering beneath warm skin.

When we finally broke apart, I was breathless. "That was..."

"Yeah." He pressed his forehead to mine. "I've been wanting to do that since that first night on the pier."

"You were a teddy bear."

"A minor detail." He grinned. "Now, show me around this beauty's engine?"

I stepped back, grateful for the distraction. "You know about vintage VWs?"

"Harper." He gave me a look. "This is what? A '73? It was only two years old when we got shoved into that machine."

"We?" I raised my eyebrows.

"My brother Sean and our friends," he explained, the laughter draining from his face.

"The *Santa Paola Six*," I said slowly, realization setting in. "That's what Lenny called you."

Ronan nodded, turning away and moving toward my workbench. "Me, Sean, Tommy, Luke, Bruno, and Mikey." Each name echoed with his pain.

"Do you know...?" I let my words trail off.

"What happened to them?" Ronan finally turned back to me, a sad smile pulling down one side of his full lips. "I don't even know what happened to me." He cocked his head to the side. "That guy Lenny said we all disappeared at the same time. So I'm hoping that they're waiting, like I was."

"That's better than the alternative?"

He barked out a laugh. "Either they're stuffed animals or they're all old men by now."

"Right." I laughed. "Sometimes I forget you're technically old enough to be my grandfather."

"Hey, now." He picked up a socket wrench. "I was cursed in suspended animation. I'm still twenty-seven."

"Whatever you say, grampa." I hip-checked him as I moved past to open Betty's engine compartment.

"Though I guess that explains why you're so good with your hands."

His eyebrows shot up. "Was that innuendo, Miss Brinkman?"

"Nope." I bent over the engine, hoping he couldn't see my blush. "Just commenting on your mechanical abilities."

"Uh huh." He stepped up behind me, reaching around to scoop up the carburetor. "Well, in that case, let me show you a thing or two about proper throttle response."

We worked side by side as the sun set, trading stories and tools. He told me about growing up in Santa Paola, about his friends who were cursed with him, about watching the world change from his glass prison on the boardwalk.

"The hardest part was the music," he said, installing a new gasket. "Watching people walk by with these tiny music players, hearing snippets of songs I didn't recognize."

"Must have been weird seeing technology evolve."

"You have no idea." He shook his head. "First time I saw someone talking on a cell phone I thought they were crazy. Just walking down the street having a conversation with thin air."

I laughed. "Wait until you see the Internet."

Eight

"I can't believe I let you talk me into this," I muttered as Quinn dragged me through the convention center doors on Sunday morning. A wave of stale air conditioning and the BO of hundreds of conspiracy theorists washed over me.

"It'll be fun!" Quinn bounced on her toes, her "I Want To Believe" t-shirt glittering with silver sequins. "Plus, Chief Hudson said we should stick together and you spent all day yesterday holed up in your house alone."

"Hmm." My gaze slid away from hers. I hadn't exactly been alone. "I'm pretty sure he meant at home, not at Nerd-Con."

"SPConCon," Quinn corrected primly. "And look how many witnesses are here if Douchebag Derek shows up."

She had a point. The convention center was packed with people wandering between booths selling everything from crystal pendulums to alien autopsy photographs. A guy in a tinfoil hat rushed past us, clutching what looked like an old fashioned radio.

"Fine." I squared my shoulders. "But I'm not buying any UFO merch."

"Deal." Quinn looped her arm through mine. "Let's go see Lenny's exhibit about the Santa Paola Six. He said it's really good this year."

The display took up an entire corner of the convention hall. Glass cases held an impressive array of vintage items and photographs. And there, front and center, was the Triumph.

"Beautiful, isn't she?" Lenny materialized behind Quinn, who jumped.

"Jesus, Lenny." She pressed a hand to her chest. "Warn a girl."

"Sorry!" He adjusted his glasses, practically vibrating with enthusiasm. "I just love sharing the mystery with new people. Did you know that all six bikes were found completely intact? Not a scratch on them."

"Really?" I moved closer to the Triumph, studying the pristine chrome. My fingers itched to touch it again.

My eyes caught on an old newspaper article mounted on the wall. The headline screamed "GANG LINKED TO SUSPICIOUS FIRE." Below it was a grainy photograph of six men lounging against vintage motorcycles, posing before a brick wall.

I stepped closer. The man in the center was unmistakably Ronan, with the same devastating smile. His arms were crossed over his chest, showing off the distinctive tattoo that wrapped around his bicep.

"That's him, Ronan O'Neill," Lenny pointed out, tapping the glass. "This was his bike. Ignore that article, though. They were framed."

"Framed?" The word escaped before I could stop it.

"My old man thought so." Chief Hudson's gruff voice joined the conversation and he appeared at my elbow, peering at the display over my shoulder. "I was just a kid, but my dad was Chief back then and he said those accusations didn't hold water."

I pulled out my phone, snapping a quick photo of the article. "What do you mean?"

The chief's weathered face creased. "They were good guys. Sure, they were a little rough around the edges, but they ran a good garage and kept their noses clean." He popped another antacid.

"Why did people think they were involved in the fire?" I asked, skimming the article. "Wait. This says the fire was at Johnson's Garage?"

Quinn elbowed us both out of the way to get a closer look at the article. "Our Johnson's Garage?"

"Your grandfather's," the Chief confirmed. "The fire burned it straight down to the ground and he had to rebuild the whole thing from scratch."

"Wow." Quinn shook her head. "I can't believe I didn't know about that."

"I'm surprised your grandmother isn't still complaining about the trouble it caused. Ronan's was the only other garage in town at the time. With those boys gone, your granddad had to fix cars out of his house for months."

"That's why some people blamed Ronan. If the Six hadn't disappeared the same night, their garage would have done a ton of business. It's our town's greatest mystery," Lenny sighed. He leaned in close, lowering his voice. "Some say they were abducted by aliens."

Quinn's eyes went wide. "Really?"

"No," Chief Hudson said flatly, popping another antacid into his mouth.

I glanced at Quinn, who was looking at Lenny with wide eyes. He nodded his head, mouthing yes, and Quinn's own mouth fell open.

"Um..." I hooked my arm through Quinn's. "Well, that's fascinating! Thanks, Lenny. We'd better keep moving if we want to see all of the exhibits."

I had to practically drag Quinn away, the Chief falling into step beside us.

"I wanted to check in with you, Miss Brinkman," he said, walking on the other side of Quinn, who was un-characteristically quiet. "Anymore sightings of Mr. Du-fort in Santa Paola?"

I shook my head. "Not that I know of," I told him. "But this is the first time I've been out of the house all weekend. Quinn insisted." I nudged her with a smile.

She gave me a distracted half smile back, but didn't say anything.

"That's good," the Chief confirmed. "He isn't staying at either of the hotels in town, but a lot of folks rent their places on those short-term websites over convention weekend." He scanned the crowd with a frown. "We're overwhelmed with nuisance calls, but I want you to know we're keeping our eyes open."

A couple walked by wearing animal costumes, covered from head to tail, and the Chief popped another antacid. "We've got a furry convention here this week-end, too."

My little blue cottage welcomed me with familiar scents—laundry detergent, fresh paint, and the lingering aroma of this morning's coffee. I kicked off my shoes, hearing them thunk against the wall as I dropped my purse on the kitchen counter.

"Ronan?" I called. "Are you—?"

Alive? Human? I wasn't sure what I was asking so the words ended abruptly, echoing into the silence.

I was disappointed but not surprised to find a teddy bear propped up against a throw pillow on the couch.

"Hi," I said awkwardly.

The bear just stared back at me with glassy green eyes.

"Ronan?" I stepped into my living room and flipped on the lights. Shadows scattered to the corners as I dumped my bag on the coffee table. "I know you can hear me in there."

But the bear remained stuffed and inanimate. I plucked him from the couch and set him on the kitchen counter while I made myself a snack. The bear toppled over, almost face-planting into my sandwich.

"Very dignified," I said, righting him again.

He stared blankly into the middle distance, ignoring me.

"Fine," I sighed, biting into my PB&J. "Be that way. But I learned some pretty interesting stuff today."

Silence.

"And I saw a picture of you from 1975. And your gang."

The bear remained stubbornly silent.

"Alright, I'm going to bed." I scooped him up and tucked him under my arm.

"The minute you pop back to human form, we need to talk." I narrowed my eyes at the bear. "You'd better not be some kind of hallucination. I will be pissed."

Warmth surrounded me, a familiar weight against my back and warm breath tickling my ear.

"Harper," a sleepy voice rumbled against my hair.

I turned in Ronan's arms to find his face inches from mine, his green eyes heavy-lidded with sleep. His bare arm was thrown across my waist, pressing me against the solid wall of his chest.

"How long have you been...awake?" I asked, my voice morning-rough.

"All night." His lips curved into that devastating half-smile. "You snore."

"I do not!" I swatted his shoulder, my palm connecting with warm, bare skin.

"Just a little," he teased, his fingers tracing lazy patterns on my skin through my t-shirt. "It's cute."

The morning sun slanted through my sheer curtains, painting golden stripes across his face. His dark hair was adorably mussed, sticking up at odd angles. Without thinking, I reached up to smooth it down, my fingers sliding through the soft strands.

Ronan caught my wrist, pressing a gentle kiss to my palm. "Morning breath and all, I still want to kiss you."

"That's the most romantic thing anyone's ever said to me," I laughed, but my stomach did a little flip.

"I aim to please." He leaned forward, closing the distance between us.

His lips were soft and warm, the kiss gentle and unhurried. His hand slid up to cup my cheek, thumb stroking my cheekbone with a tenderness that made my chest ache. When he pulled back, his smile was dazzling.

"That was nice," I whispered.

"Mmm," he agreed, pulling me closer until we were a tangle of limbs. "This is nice too. Just being here with you."

I rested my head against his chest, listening to the steady thump of his heart. "Were you really up all night?"

Ronan sighed, "No, not really. I sleep a lot when I'm shifted." His gaze met mine. "I don't want to miss a second of being human, but the temptation to fall asleep with you in my arms is too great."

"You can't control the shift at all?"

"Not yet. I still haven't figured out the rules." His fingers traced up and down my spine, raising goosebumps in their wake. "All magic has rules."

"Well, this is nice." I snuggled deeper into his embrace. "Even if it's temporary."

"Very nice," he agreed, his voice dropping an octave as his hand slid lower to rest at the curve of my hip. "Though now that I think about it, no one's shared a bed with me in..." He paused. "Fifty years, give or take."

"Poor baby," I teased, tapping his nose with my finger. "Fifty years of celibacy."

His eyes darkened. "It feels like much longer with you pressing against me like this."

A delicious shiver ran through me. "I should probably get up and start getting ready for work." I made no move to leave his arms. "Soon."

"Soon," he agreed, his thumb now tracing the strip of skin where my t-shirt had ridden up.

"The convention!" I sat up suddenly, nearly smacking him in the chin. "I almost forgot!"

Ronan laughed, propping himself up on one elbow to watch me scramble off the bed.

"I found out so much," I said, digging through yesterday's jeans for my phone. "There was this whole exhibit about you."

"About me?" He sat up fully now, the sheet pooling around his waist—and thank God for that sheet, because apparently Ronan was still as naked as the day he was born.

Focus, Harper.

"You and your friends. The Santa Paola Six," I confirmed, triumphantly holding up my phone. "Lenny had a whole display. Did you know my garage burned down the night you all disappeared? And some people thought you guys were involved."

Ronan's face darkened. "We didn't burn down the garage."

"I know that," I said quickly, climbing back into bed and scooting next to him. "Chief Hudson was there and he said his dad never believed it either."

I pulled up the photo I'd taken of the newspaper article, holding it out to him. Ronan looked at the device in my hand with open fascination. "You can zoom in like this."

His face grew serious as he studied the newspaper article and photo. His finger traced over the image of himself and his friends, posed in front of their motorcycles.

"That's us," he said quietly. "God, this feels like yesterday." His thumb brushed over each face in turn. "That's my little brother Sean. And that's Tommy, the clean cut guy. He was going to be a school teacher. The big guy is Bruno. You can't tell in this picture, but Luke's a redhead." His voice grew softer. "And Mikey, angry at the world as usual."

The pain in his voice tightened my throat and I took his hand, threading our fingers together. "Tell me about them."

Ronan handed me back the phone and leaned back against the headboard, pulling me against his side. "Sean is an artist."

"He looks like you," I pointed out, zooming into Sean's picture.

Ronan ran a finger over the screen and it flipped to the camera app, showing his own face. He jumped, startled.

"See," I pointed out with a smile. "Same hair. Did Sean have green eyes too?"

He stared at his own reflection, tapping the screen. "Yes, just like our mom's. She was a painter, too. Sean should have been in LA, making a name for himself, but since our parents died he refused to leave me here alone."

"You miss him," I said softly.

"I miss all of them. Every day." His arm tightened around me. "It should've been only me."

"What do you mean?"

He shook his head. "It's my fault they got caught up in everything. The garage, the trouble, the fire—all of it." His jaw tightened. "I made bad choices and they paid for them too."

I turned to face him fully. "Hey, look at me." I waited until his eyes met mine. "Whatever happened, I'm willing to bet they wouldn't blame you."

"You don't know what I did."

"No, but I know who you are." I placed my palm against his cheek. "And that matters more."

Something shifted in his expression, a vulnerability I hadn't seen before. His hand came up to cover mine.

"How do you do that?" he murmured.

"Do what?"

"See through all my bullshit."

I smiled. "Mechanic, remember? I'm good at figuring out what's under the hood."

He laughed, the sound rumbling through his chest. "That was terrible."

"Made you laugh, though," I pointed out.

His eyes crinkled at the corners. "Yeah."

The moment stretched between us, charged with possibility. His gaze dropped to my mouth, and my heart kicked against my ribs.

"I'm going to kiss you again," he whispered.

"Okay," I breathed.

This kiss wasn't gentle. It was heat and need and fifty years of waiting. His hands tangled in my hair, pulling me closer as his mouth claimed mine. I melted against him, my fingers digging into the solid muscle of his shoulders.

When we broke apart, gasping for air, his eyes had darkened to midnight. "Harper," he groaned, his voice rough. "Tell me to stop if this isn't what you want."

In answer, I pulled my t-shirt over my head and tossed it aside.

His sharp intake of breath sent a thrill through me. His gaze traveled over me with such reverence that I forgot to be self-conscious.

"You're beautiful," he whispered, his hand hovering just above my skin as if he was afraid to touch. "So damn beautiful."

I guided his hand to my breast. "You can touch me, you know."

His palm was rough with calluses as it cupped my breast, his thumb brushing across my nipple. The contact sent electricity shooting down my spine, drawing a gasp from my lips.

"Like that?" he asked, a hint of smugness in his voice.

"Shut up and kiss me," I demanded.

He laughed, a deep, rich sound that vibrated through me where our bodies pressed together. Then his mouth was on mine, and talking became the last thing on my mind.

His lips trailed from my mouth to my jaw, then down my neck, leaving fire in their wake. Every touch was gentle but insistent, as if he couldn't quite believe I was real.

"Is this okay?" he murmured against my collarbone.

"More than okay," I assured him, letting my head fall back to give him better access.

His mouth moved lower, replacing his hand on my breast. The first touch of his tongue against my nipple had me arching off the bed, a moan escaping my lips.

"God, the sounds you make," he groaned, his hand sliding down my stomach to the edge of my underwear. "Can I?"

"Yes," I breathed, lifting my hips to help him slide them down my legs.

His fingers explored me with maddening slowness, discovering what made me gasp and tremble. When one finger slipped inside me, I nearly came off the bed.

"Easy," he soothed, his mouth returning to mine for a deep, drugging kiss. "We've got all the time in the world."

"I have to be at work in two hours," I reminded him, my hand sliding down to wrap around him.

It was his turn to gasp, his hips jerking forward into my touch. "Keep that up and this will be over embarrassingly fast."

I grinned against his mouth. "Can't have that."

He moved over me, his weight supported on his forearms. His eyes locked with mine, suddenly serious. "You're sure about this?"

In answer, I wrapped my legs around his waist, bringing him to my entrance. "I've never been more sure of anything."

The first press of him inside me stole my breath. He moved slowly, giving me time to adjust, his eyes never leaving mine. When he was fully seated, he stilled, his forehead coming to rest against mine.

"You feel like heaven," he whispered.

"Move," I urged, rolling my hips up to meet his.

He didn't need to be told twice. His strokes were deep and measured, each one hitting something inside me that made stars burst behind my eyelids. My nails raked down his back, urging him on.

"Harper," he groaned, his rhythm faltering. "I can't—"

"Let go," I whispered, biting gently at his earlobe. "I've got you."

His release triggered waves of pleasure that crashed over me as he buried his face in my neck, my name a prayer on his lips.

Afterward, we lay tangled together, sweat cooling on our skin. Ronan traced lazy patterns on my hip, his expression one of wonder.

"So," I finally said, breaking the silence. "Was that was worth waiting fifty years for?"

His laugh shook us both. "I would've waited a hundred." He pressed a kiss to my temple. "Though I'm glad I didn't have to."

I snuggled closer, savoring the warmth of him. "You know what this means, right?"

"That I need to figure out how to stay human?" he guessed.

"That too. But I was thinking of those pants I bought you." I grinned up at him. "Complete waste of money."

His smile was brighter than the morning sun streaming through my window. "I'll make it up to you," he promised, pulling me in for another kiss.

"I'm counting on it," I murmured against his lips.

Nine

I smiled down into the engine of Lenny's Wrangler as Quinn paced along the center aisle of the garage, waving her arms like she was directing airplane traffic.

"But why would anyone think the Santa Paola Six had something to do with burning down our garage?" She stopped abruptly, planting her hands on her hips. "That makes zero sense, Dad. Everyone always talks about them like they were local heroes!"

Frank Johnson didn't look up from the engine he was tuning. "No one really thought that, honey. We were all pretty sure it was Benny Boots. He was trouble."

"Betty Boop?" Quinn stopped abruptly in the middle of the garage, her arms falling to her side as she stared at her father's back in confusion.

Frank emerged from the car he was working on with a frustrated sigh. "Benny Boots," he corrected. "He was the loan shark who had given Ronan O'Niell the money to start his garage."

"Wait, what?" Quinn's voice hit a note only dogs could hear. "You never mentioned a loan shark!"

I bit my lip to hide my smile. Quinn had been on this tear since she'd walked in two hours ago, interrogating her father about a fifty-year-old fire.

"It was fifty years ago." Frank's expression remained impassive. "Must've slipped my mind."

Quinn threw her hands in the air. "We have loan sharks in Santa Paola? Is this guy still alive? Did they ever catch him?"

"It was a long time ago, Quinn." Frank said, his weathered face unreadable. "Keep in mind, I was just a kid myself. I wasn't even working here then."

"But—"

"Just a loose gasket in the Wrangler," I interrupted, wiping my hands on a shop rag. "But I'm going to need to order the part."

Frank nodded, clearly relieved by the change of subject. "Shouldn't take long, but I'll let Lenny know."

Quinn wasn't so easily deterred. "Dad—"

"Speaking of the time," I jumped in again, "who's ready for lunch?"

Quinn's head whipped toward me. "Lunch?"

Frank sent me a grateful nod. "You girls should take a break and go over to the diner for lunch."

I sent Frank a wink and threaded my arm through Quinn's. "That's a great idea," I said as I dragged her toward the door. "Can we bring you back anything, Frank?"

He waved us off, sagging in relief. "No, I'm good. Take your time."

I giggled softly, bouncing out the door and onto the sidewalk. "You know what I want?" I asked Quinn.

"What?" Quinn asked, dazed by our abrupt exit.

"One of Agatha's cinnamon rolls!" I answered with a smile.

Quinn's attention snapped to me, her eyes narrowing. "You look..."

I nearly tripped over a crack in the sidewalk. "What?"

"Happy." She studied my face with suspicion. "You look happy."

Heat crept up my neck. "Of course I'm happy, we're going to lunch."

Quinn's eyes widened. "Oh my god, you got laid!"

"What?" My voice came out two octaves higher than normal.

"You got laid!" Quinn bounced on her toes. "Who is he? When did this happen? Why didn't you tell me?"

"Oh my god, stop,'" I insisted. "We are not having this conversation on a public sidewalk."

"Fine." Quinn grabbed my arm. "We'll have it over lunch. Come on."

The bell above the door of the diner jangled as Quinn frog marched me inside, the smell of grilled onions and coffee immediately enveloping us. The vinyl booths squeaked as we slid into our usual spot by the window.

"Spill," Quinn demanded the second our butts hit the seats.

I grabbed a menu even though I knew it by heart. "There's nothing to spill."

"Harper Brinkman." Quinn snatched the menu from my hands and slapped it onto the counter with unnec-essary force. "I have known you since freshman orienta-tion. I have held you while you cried and held your hair while you puked. I know when you're lying. And I know when you've been thoroughly and properly fu—"

"Quinn!" I glanced around, relieved to see the lunch crowd was focused on their meals.

"Well?" She leaned forward, eyebrows raised.

"Fine." I sighed, twisting a paper napkin into a rope. "I...met someone."

Her squeal nearly shattered the windows. "I knew it! Who is he? Do I know him? Is he hot? On a scale of one to ten, how good was it?"

"He's new in town. Kind of," I hedged. "And yes, he's hot. Very hot." My cheeks burned at the memory of Ronan's body moving above mine.

"And?" Quinn prompted.

"And that's all you're getting."

"Boo, you whore." She pouted, then brightened. "Is it serious? Or just a fun rebound from Douchebag Derek?"

I opened my mouth to answer when Agatha appeared at my elbow in her usual black tee featuring the diner's logo.

"Hey, guys. The usual?" She plucked the pencil tucked into her short black bob and held it ready over her order pad.

"Yes, please," I said gratefully. "How's the van running?"

"Purring like a kitten," Agatha confirmed. "You want any sides with your burger?"

"I'll have the fries." I added with a smile, "Can I get one of your cinnamon rolls to take back to the shop with me?"

She made a notation on her pad. "Sure thing, Harper. Heart attack on a plate, Quinnie?"

"Yes, sir," Quinn answered with a salute. "Extra heart attack on the side."

Quinn waggled her eyebrows at me as Agatha tucked the pencil back behind her ear and walked away. "Worked up an appetite, did you?"

I kicked her under the table.

"Ow! Fine, keep your secrets." She sipped her water. "But I'm happy for you, Harper. You deserve someone who doesn't suck."

The sincerity in her voice made my throat tight. "Thanks, Quinn."

"And if he hurts you, I'll murder him and make it look like an accident."

I laughed. "I have no doubt."

"Speaking of accidents waiting to happen..." Quinn's expression darkened as she looked past me.

The warm glow I'd held inside me all morning disappeared as a chill raced up my spine.

"Harper." Derek's voice sliced through the diner chatter.

Quinn's eyes narrowed to slits. "You're not welcome here, DD. Go away."

I turned my head slowly, my breath frozen in my chest. The man I'd thought I'd loved stood beside our booth. He looked exactly the same—perfect hair, perfect clothes. His handsome face broke into that charming smile that had once made my heart race. Now it just made my skin crawl.

Derek ignored Quinn, his attention fixed on me. "I've missed you so much." His voice dropped to that intimate tone he used when he wanted something. "I know I made a mistake. You have every right to be angry, but running away isn't the answer."

"I didn't run away," I said evenly. "I left. There's a difference."

His smile tightened. "You're splitting hairs. The point is, we belong together. This little rebellion has gone on long enough."

"Rebellion?" Quinn's voice rose. "She's not a teenager who missed curfew, DD. She left because you hit her!"

The background noise of the diner cut off as if someone had flipped a switch and a sea of heads turned our way.

Derek's jaw clenched. "Don't call me that."

"Should I call you by your full legal name, Douchebag Derek?" Quinn sneered.

Derek's smile was completely gone now. He swung his focus to Quinn and I could breathe again. "That's not my name," he growled at her.

"If you don't want to be called a douchebag, you should stop being one," Quinn pointed out, poking at the bear one time too many.

Derek's hands hit the table with a crash and I jumped, my heart stuttering. "It was a misunderstanding!" he roared into her face.

My muscles unfroze and I pushed out of the booth and rose smoothly to my feet. I was mere inches from Derek, but my heartbeat had evened out. "Get away from her," I told him calmly. "We're leaving."

He swung back toward me and his hand snapped out to wrap around my wrist like a cobra striking. "You're not going anywhere until we sort this out."

"Let go of me," I said firmly as Quinn scrambled out of the booth to stand at my side.

"Not until you listen to reason. I told you, this was all a misunderstanding."

"We all understand exactly what you are, DD," Quinn stated firmly, wedging herself between us.

"The lady asked you to let go." Dan from the hardware store appeared beside our table, arms crossed over his barrel chest.

Derek's eyes flickered to Dan, then back to me. "This is a private conversation."

"Not anymore, it isn't." Agatha appeared with our food, reaching around Derek to set her tray down on our now empty table. She unloaded the plates and Quinn's glass, then grabbed my mug of coffee and set it down right at the edge of the table with enough force that hot coffee sloshed over the rim and onto Derek's pressed khakis.

"Shit!" He jumped back, releasing my wrist to brush at the stain blossoming across the front of his pants. "Look what you did, you stupid bitch!"

"Oh, no." Agatha didn't look remotely sorry. "Clumsy me."

"I think you'd better leave, young man," Mrs. Peterson advised, stepping up into the opening as Quinn pushed me back away from Derek.

"This is ridiculous." Derek's handsome face twisted with anger as he glared at me over Quinn's head. "Harper, tell these people to mind their own business."

"This is our business." The other waitress, an older woman named Cleo with a teased red updo, came to stand beside Agatha. "We take care of our own in Santa Paola." A murmur of agreement rippled around the room and other diners moved to their feet.

Derek's expression smoothed into that charming mask I knew too well.

"I apologize for the disturbance." He pulled out his wallet and dropped a twenty on the table. "For the coffee."

As he moved toward the door, he paused beside me. "This isn't over," he murmured, low enough that only I could hear. "You can't hide behind these small-town hicks forever. We're meant to be together, Harper. One way or another."

Then he was gone, the bell jangling cheerfully as the door closed behind him.

Ten

I pushed my front door closed with my hip, balancing a stack of takeout containers in my arms like the world's greasiest game of Jenga. The smell of sweet and sour chicken wafted up, making my stomach growl in anticipation.

"Honey, I'm home," I called out hopefully.

The living room lights clicked on, and there he stood, barefoot in a pair of sweatpants and nothing else. His dark hair was rumpled, as if he'd been running his hands through it, and his smile—that crooked, devastating smile—made my heart do an Olympic-level gymnastics routine in my chest.

"Hi," I said softly, making no attempt to hide my dumb smile.

"Hi," he said, moving closer and pulling the boxes of food from my hands. "I just shifted about five minutes ago."

"Lucky me." We stood too close together, his green eyes impossibly deep. "Chinese food okay?"

"Chinese food is wonderful," he said, the corners of his full lips turning up.

Ronan finally moved away and a sigh left my body in relief and disappointment. I was right on his heels as he moved to the kitchen and set the containers on the counter. When he turned to face me, his expression shifted as he took in my face.

"What's wrong?" he asked, reaching for my hand. "Did something happen today?"

"That obvious, huh?" I sank into a kitchen chair.

Ronan pulled another chair close and sat, knee to knee with me. "You look like you're about to vibrate out of your skin."

I blew out a long breath. "Derek showed up at the diner while Quinn and I were having lunch."

His whole body went rigid, muscles coiling like springs. "What did he do?"

"Nothing." I placed my hand on his knee, feeling his thundering pulse beneath my palm. "He grabbed my wrist, but that was it."

A muscle jumped in Ronan's jaw. "That's enough."

"The entire diner had my back," I continued, squeezing his knee. "Dan from the hardware store stepped in, and Agatha 'accidentally' spilled coffee on Derek's crotch." A small smile tugged at my lips despite the lingering tension in my shoulders. "Everyone gave him hell, even Mrs. Peterson. It was awesome."

Ronan's expression softened slightly. "This town always did look after its own."

"That's exactly what Cleo said."

"Smart lady." He captured my hand, running his thumb over my knuckles. "When my parents died and I was left raising Sean, our neighbors would drop off casseroles without a word."

I leaned my back against the chair, the tension of the day starting to fade. "It's kind of amazing. They barely know me, but they all jumped to my defense."

"Some things don't change." Ronan smiled, a hint of sadness in his eyes. "The buildings may look a little different, the cars are a little sleeker, the clothes are... well, I'm still getting used to yoga pants." His gaze dropped briefly to my legs. "But the heart of this place—that's the same."

"What was it like?" I asked. "Growing up here?"

"Simpler, in some ways." He looked past me, into memories I couldn't see. "We didn't have much, but we had the ocean and each other. Sean and I used to race our bikes down the boardwalk at night after the tourists had all gone home." His smile widened. "Mrs. Peterson was old even then."

"Wait—the same Mrs. Peterson? She was old fifty years ago?" I straightened up. "How is that possible?"

Ronan shrugged. "Maybe it's magic?"

"Says the cursed teddy bear?" I pointed out, with an arched eyebrow.

"Exactly." Ronan stood, pulling me up with him. "Let's eat before the food gets cold. I'm starving."

Ronan moved to grab plates, but I caught his wrist, tugging him back to me. His eyes darkened as I pressed myself against him.

"Thank you," I whispered.

"For what?"

"For listening. For being here." I stretched up on my toes.

His hands cupped my face as he bent to meet me halfway. The kiss was soft at first, a gentle press of his lips against mine, but it quickly deepened. One of his hands slid to the small of my back, pressing me closer as his tongue swept into my mouth, tasting of mint and something uniquely Ronan.

I pulled away to smile up at him in bemusement. "Did you use my toothbrush?"

Color flooded along Ronan's cheekbones and the tops of his ears. "Umm..." he mumbled.

A delighted laugh bubbled out of me and I pressed it into his mouth. My tongue swept across his teeth, chasing the minty taste as I wound my arms around his neck, pressing up against his bare chest. The heat of his skin seeped through my thin t-shirt, warming me from the outside in. My fingers tangled in his hair as his hand slipped under the hem of my shirt, calloused fingertips skimming along my spine.

A knock at the door made me jump, and Ronan froze.

"Harper? It's me!" Quinn's voice called through the door. "I brought wine and my sleeping bag!"

Ronan's eyes widened in panic. "Sleeping bag?" he mouthed.

"Oh no," I whispered back, my hands flying up to fix my hair.

"I can hear you whispering in there!" Quinn called. "If you've got a guy in there, I swear to God—"

Before I could respond, Ronan was gone. One second I was holding a very sexy, very human man—the next I had my arms wrapped around a teddy bear.

"Dammit," I muttered, staring down at the stuffed toy in my arms.

Juggling the bear in one arm, I yanked open the front door to find Quinn holding up a bottle of wine triumphantly.

"You have the worst timing," I told her with a sigh.

"I come bearing gifts!" She announced, then stopped short, her eyes dropping to the teddy bear clutched to my chest. "And I see you're already having a party with Mr. Cuddles."

"His name is Ronan," I corrected automatically, stepping back to let her in.

Quinn breezed past me, heading straight for the kitchen. "Ooh, Chinese! Did you get those little dumpling things I like?"

"Yes, your highness." I set Ronan carefully on the couch and followed her.

"So," Quinn poured two generous glasses of wine and handed me one. "You want to tell me more about this mystery man who has you glowing like radioactive waste?"

I choked on my first sip. "I'm not glowing."

"Honey, you're practically Godzilla attacking Tokyo." She hopped onto the counter, swinging her legs. "Spill."

I busied myself opening containers. "There's not much to tell. He's...different."

"Different how? Three nipples? Extra toe? Republican?"

"No! God, no." I laughed despite myself. "He's just..." My laughter faded. I had no idea where to go from here. I definitely didn't want to lie to Quinn, but...

Quinn's eyes grew round. "Oh my god, he isn't married, is he?"

"Of course not," I replied, scandalized.

"Criminal record?"

"No!"

"Then what's with the secrecy?" She hopped down and loaded a plate with food. "Why can't I meet him?"

"He's shy," I said lamely, following her to the living room.

Quinn plopped down on the couch next to the bear. She picked him up and set him on her lap, patting his head absently.

"Cute bear." She poked his glass eye. "But you're changing the subject."

I stared at Ronan helplessly, wondering if he could feel Quinn manhandling him. "Let's talk about something else. Like, how about that scene Derek caused today?"

"Nice deflection." Quinn pointed her fork at me. "But I'll allow it because watching Agatha dump coffee on DD's crotch was the highlight of my year."

"Mine too," I admitted, settling into the armchair. "I just wish I knew why he won't give up. We were together for two years, and he spent most of that time telling me everything I did wrong."

Quinn snorted. "Because he's a controlling asshat who can't stand that you slipped his leash."

"I guess." I pushed a dumpling around my plate. "Sometimes I can't believe I stayed with him as long as I did."

"Love makes us stupid," Quinn said sagely. "But you got smart quick when he crossed the line." Quinn set Ronan aside and leaned forward, her eyes fierce. "This whole town has your back. And so does your new mystery man, I'm sure."

I glanced at Ronan, who had tipped over on the couch cushion. "Yeah, I think he does."

"So..." Quinn's voice turned sly. "About this guy. Is he good in bed?"

"Quinn!" I threw a fortune cookie at her head.

"Valid question!" She caught it easily. "On a scale of 'is it in yet' to 'holy mother of God', where does he fall?"

Heat flooded my face as memories of Ronan's hands and mouth on my body flashed through my mind. "None of your business."

"That good, huh?" Quinn grinned triumphantly. "I knew it!"

"Can we please talk about something else?"

Quinn relented, switching to gossip about the garage and Frank's latest silent feud with the UPS guy. All the while, I kept stealing glances at Ronan.

After three glasses of wine and half a pint of ice cream, Quinn finally yawned and stretched. "I'm calling it. You ready for bed?"

"Yup," I confirmed, gathering our dishes. "I'll be in soon."

Quinn paused at the hallway, her expression softening. "I'm glad you're happy, Harper. You deserve it." Her eyes flickered to the teddy bear on the couch. "Though you might want to upgrade from Mr. Cuddles to an actual human boyfriend soon."

If only she knew.

"Night, Quinn," I said, smiling innocently.

After she disappeared down the hall, I scooped Ronan up and whispered, "If you have any control over your shift, keep it in your pants tonight, buddy."

The bear stared back blankly, but I could have sworn his glass eyes twinkled with amusement.

"Yeah, yeah. Laugh it up." I tucked him under my arm. "Let's go to bed."

Eleven

"Oh my god. Oh my god. Oh. My. GOD."

Quinn's voice pierced through the thick fog of my dreams, each repetition hammering another nail into the coffin of my beautiful sleep. I groaned and burrowed deeper under my blankets, hoping that if I ignored her, she'd go away.

She did not go away.

"You pervert!" A pillow smacked into my head. "Wake up!"

I pried one eye open, the moonlight filtering through my curtains just bright enough to make out Quinn's silhouette. She knelt beside my bed, her sleeping bag bunched up beneath her and her red hair sticking out in every direction.

"Whassit?" I mumbled, my tongue thick with sleep. "Fire? Earthquake? Zombie apocalypse?"

"Harper Brinkman, you absolute deviant."

I propped myself up on one elbow, my brain still half-submerged in dreamland. "Wha—?"

The bedside lamp clicked on, flooding the room with light that stabbed directly into my retinas. I hissed like a vampire at a tanning salon and threw my arm over my eyes.

"You're boinking a teddy bear."

My heart stopped.

Quinn stood over me, her red hair a spectacular disaster, with Ronan clutched in her hands like incriminating evidence. Her eyes were as wide as dinner plates.

"I...what?" Brilliant response, Harper. Truly inspired.

"Your. Boyfriend. Is. A. Teddy. Bear." Quinn punctuated each word by shaking Ronan slightly. His little plush head wobbled back and forth, green glass eyes gleaming in the lamplight. "Not metaphorically. Literally."

The last cobwebs of sleep vanished from my brain as adrenaline flooded my system. "That's crazy," I stammered, reaching for Ronan. "Give him back."

Quinn yanked him out of reach. "Oh no! You've been cuddling up with this little guy for days. I was getting worried about you, but I had no idea!"

"It's just a toy. It's completely normal!" My voice rose into what could generously be called a squeak.

"People don't whisper sweet nothings to toys and call them by real names." Quinn held Ronan up to eye level, examining him with narrowed eyes. "Real names of real humans who disappeared under mysterious circumstances."

I swallowed hard. "I think you're reading way too much into—"

"Shut up," Quinn interrupted, not unkindly. "I know I'm right." She tapped her temple with her free hand. "It's intuition, baby."

"Intuition that my boyfriend is a stuffed animal?" I tried for skeptical but landed somewhere closer to panicked.

"Yes! Exactly!" Quinn bounced in her sleeping bag. "I'm glad you aren't still trying to hide it!"

"I'm not trying to hide it because there's nothing to hide." I lunged for Ronan again.

Quinn scrambled backward, holding Ronan over her head. "Then why are you so desperate to get your hands on this bear, huh?"

"Because you're manhandling him!" The sentence escaped before I could stop it.

Quinn froze, a triumphant grin spreading across her face. "Him. Not 'it.' Him."

Oh damn.

We stared at each other in the lamplight, Quinn victorious, me caught with my metaphorical pants down.

"Fine," I groaned, flopping back onto my pillow. "You win."

"I knew it!" Quinn shrieked, bouncing so hard she nearly toppled over. "I freaking KNEW IT! This is the most amazing thing that's ever happened to me. My best friend is dating a werebear!"

"He's not a *werebear*. That's not even a real thing," I hissed, pulling the blankets over my head.

The edge of my mattress dipped as Quinn climbed up, yanking the covers back and inserting herself into my bed. "Explain. Now. Everything." When I just stared at her blankly she dangled Ronan in my direction. "If you want your boytoy back, start talking."

I sat up, hugging my knees to my chest, and stared at Ronan's immobile form in Quinn's grip. His sewn-on smile seemed more resigned than usual.

"He's not always a bear," I started, each word feeling like I was stepping off a cliff without knowing how far down the ground was. "Sometimes he's human."

Quinn's eyes narrowed. "And *he* is Ronan O'Neill, right?"

"Right." I ran a hand through my tangled hair. "He's... cursed."

"Cursed," Quinn repeated, testing the word out. "Like fairy tale cursed? Beauty and the Beast style?"

"I guess." I blew out a long breath.

Quinn's gaze snapped to the teddy bear, which remained stubbornly inanimate. "Holy shit buckets." She shook him gently. "Ronan? Can you hear me in there? Blink once for yes, twice for no."

"It doesn't work like that," I said, reaching for him again. This time Quinn handed him over without resistance. I cradled Ronan against my chest, smoothing his fur where Quinn had ruffled it. "He can hear and see everything, but he can't move or speak in bear form."

"So he's just trapped?" Quinn's excitement faded slightly. "That's actually kind of horrible."

"Yeah," I agreed softly, running my thumb over Ronan's plush ear. "It is."

"But when is he human? How does it work?" Quinn leaned forward, her knees pressing into mine through the blankets. "I need details, woman!"

I sighed, wondering how to explain something I barely understood myself. "I really have no idea. It's unpredictable. He seems to shift when I need him, or when we're alone. But if he's startled, or if someone else shows up unexpectedly..."

"Poof! Instant stuffie!" Quinn snapped her fingers.

"Pretty much," I agreed.

Quinn's brow furrowed. "So all those times you were acting weird and secretive..."

"Yup."

"And the mystery boyfriend..."

"Is Ronan."

"And the sex..."

"Is phenomenal," I admitted, heat climbing my neck.

Quinn slapped her hands over her mouth, muffling a delighted squeal. "This is better than any telenovela!" She dropped her hands. "So make him change! I want to meet him—the real him!"

I shook my head. "I can't. It doesn't work like that."

"Like what? How does it work?"

"If I knew that, don't you think I would have figured out how to break the curse by now?" The frustration in my voice was unmistakable.

Quinn deflated slightly. "Right. Sorry." She brightened again almost instantly. "Did you try kissing him? That's how it works in the movies."

"We've done more than kiss, Quinn." I gave her a long side eye.

"Right." She drew out the word and crossed her arms. "Have you tried...I don't know, witchcraft? Voodoo? A really stern talking-to?"

Despite everything, a laugh bubbled up from my chest. "A stern talking-to?"

"It works on the parts supply guy!"

We dissolved into giggles, the absurdity of the situation finally hitting us both.

"So let me get this straight," Quinn said when we'd calmed down. "You're dating a cursed teddy bear who used to be the leader of a motorcycle gang fifty years ago, who randomly turns human sometimes but can't control when, and who is just a regular stuffed toy around everyone else?"

"That about sums it up, yeah."

Quinn nodded thoughtfully. "Cool. Cool cool cool."

I blinked at her. "That's it? 'Cool'? I tell you my boyfriend is a cursed teddy bear, and your response is 'cool'?"

She shrugged. "What do you want me to say? That you're crazy? That I don't believe you? That I'm going to run screaming into the night?" She reached over and patted Ronan's head. "Besides, this is the most exciting thing that's happened in this town since Mrs. Peterson flashed the mayor at last year's Founder's Day parade."

I blinked. "She what?"

Quinn shrugged. "We live in Santa Paola, Harper. This town really is kind of weird."

Relief crashed over me like a wave, leaving me light-headed. "Thanks for not thinking I'm insane."

"Oh, I definitely think you're insane," Quinn assured me with a leer, eyebrows wiggling suggestively, "but not because of this."

"What does that mean?"

"So," Quinn said, ignoring me and poking at the bear's round belly, "you haven't answered my question. How do we make him change? I want to meet your new hottie."

I placed my hand protectively over Ronan. "I told you, I don't know. It just happens."

"Ugh, that's so inconvenient." Quinn flopped back onto my pillow. "What if we scare him? Like, say 'boo' really loud?"

I stared at her blankly.

"What about..." Quinn sat up straight, eyes wide. "Oh, I've got it! What if we try to recreate the conditions when he first changed? You know, like in the movies where they have to go back to the beginning to break the spell!"

I shrugged, my exhaustion catching up with me. "The first time was when I was sleeping. He was just there when I woke up."

"Perfect!" Quinn clapped her hands. "Let's go to sleep, and maybe he'll change!"

"With you in the room?" I raised an eyebrow. "Not likely."

Quinn's face fell. "Right. He only changes for you." She frowned at me. "And why do we think that is again?"

"He said that we're...that he thinks that I'm..." I trailed off, my cheeks getting hot.

"You're...?" Quinn prompted me. "Spill it, woman!"

I took in a deep breath, bracing myself. "His soulmate," I blurted.

Instead of bursting out into laughter, Quinn clasped her hands together, her eyes wide. "Oh my god, that's awesome," she gushed.

"It is?" I stated hopefully. "I'm not a complete loser for trusting a strange man who I just met and who sometimes becomes an inanimate object?"

"Oh, no, you definitely are," Quinn nodded sagely, "but it's also wonderful and I'm so happy for you."

I yanked the pillow out from under her and beat her with it, both of us laughing until we cried. Exhausted, we finally collapsed back on the bed with silly grins stuck on our faces.

Quinn rolled over onto her side, sandwiching her hands under her chin. "Okay, I'm going to fall asleep so that Ronan can come out to play." She closed her eyes, and let out an exaggerated snore.

"Very convincing," I deadpanned. "Oscar-worthy, really."

One eye popped open. "No good?"

"No good."

Quinn sat up with a huff. "Fine. But this isn't over. Operation BoyToy is officially a go."

"Can we please come up with a better name than 'Operation BoyToy'?"

"Absolutely not." Quinn shimmied back down into her sleeping bag. "Now, since I'm apparently not meeting him tonight, we should get some sleep. Some of us have to work in the morning."

"This conversation isn't too weird for you to sleep?" I asked, clutching Ronan closer as I frowned at her over the side of the bed.

Quinn yawned dramatically. "You know I have a very high tolerance for weird." She reached up and clicked off the lamp, plunging the room back into darkness. "G'night, Harper. G'night, Ronan."

I settled back against my pillow, Ronan tucked securely under my chin. "Night, Quinn."

In the darkness, I could almost feel Ronan's heartbeat against mine, though I knew it was just my imagination. Quinn's soft, rhythmic breathing soon filled the room.

Just before I drifted off, Quinn's drowsy voice floated up from the floor. "Hey, Harper?"

"Hmm?"

"I'm really glad you found someone who makes you happy. Even if he is sometimes small and fuzzy."

A smile spread across my face in the darkness. "Thanks, Quinn."

"But I'm going to need details about the sex eventually. Like, does he ever accidentally turn back into a bear during—"

I threw a pillow at her head. "Go to sleep, Quinn!"

Her muffled laughter followed me into my dreams.

The familiar smell of motor oil and coffee wrapped around me like a comfortable blanket as I leaned over Lenny's Wrangler. This was my happy place—metal and grease and the satisfying click of tools doing exactly what they were supposed to do.

"So, is he more of a honey or a grizzly?"

I jerked up, smacking my head against the underside of the hood with a hollow clang.

"Son of a—" I bit back the rest of the curse as I clutched at my aching head. "Quinn, what the hell?"

"What? I'm just asking an innocent question about stuffed animals." Her smile was about as innocent as a shark's.

"Nothing about you is innocent." I grabbed a shop rag to wipe my hands, wincing as I caught sight of my reflection in the side mirror. A grease was smeared across my forehead. "And you made me give myself a unicorn horn."

"It really brings out your eyes." Quinn tilted her head, examining my face with clinical detachment.

"I hate you."

"No, you don't. You love me, just like you love your bear-y special friend." She wiggled her eyebrows suggestively.

I dropped my head back with a groan that echoed off the metal walls of the garage. "Why did I tell you anything?"

"You didn't. I figured it out all on my own, remember?" Quinn stuck out her tongue and hopped up onto the workbench, kicking her legs like a five-year-old. "Besides, you're just mad because he didn't make an appearance last night."

"Keep your voice down!" I glanced nervously toward the office again.

"Fine, fine." She mimed zipping her lips, then immediately reversed the gesture and unzipped them. "But you still haven't answered my question. Honey or grizzly?"

I rolled my eyes skyward, praying for patience. "Teddy, obviously."

"Boring." Quinn reached for the wrench in my hand. "But seriously, when do I get to meet him? The real him, not the cute fuzzy version."

"I told you, I have no control over when he changes. And neither does he."

"When is the next full moon?"

"That's for werewolves, you loon." I snatched the wrench back before she could do any damage.

"And were*bears*," she corrected solemnly.

"That's not a thing!"

"How do you know? Maybe it is!" Quinn leaned forward. "Maybe your boyfriend is the first ever werebear. You could be making cryptozoological history, Harper!"

I pointed the wrench at her nose. "One more bear pun and I'll—"

The bell above the door jangled, cutting off my empty threat. Lenny's tall, gangly figure shuffled in, his plaid shirt buttoned all the way to his neck despite the early summer heat. His eyes darted around the garage before landing on me.

"Hi, Harper," he waved happily as he made his way over to me. "Hi, Quinn. I was just walking past and thought I'd poke my head in."

I wiped my hands on the shop rag again. "Hi, Lenny." Turning, I pointed at Quinn. "You. Back to work."

She flipped me off before jumping down from the bench and skipping back to her desk and I turned back to Lenny.

I waved my hand at his car. "Everything is done except for installing that part we're waiting for. It should be here any minute."

"That's great." He leaned over the engine, his eyes running over the components as a small frown bloomed between his brows. "You said the old gasket was corroded?"

"Yup." I reached for my phone from where I'd left it on the workbench. "I took a photo and meant to send it to you. Here you go." I handed him the phone displaying a closeup of the worn metal. "See how that edge is all chewed up?"

"Oh, man." Lenny's eyes got big. "That's not normal, is it?"

"Good catch." I smiled at him in approval. "That's not a normal wear and tear pattern at all. So I looked a little closer and found the problem right here—" I was turning back to the engine as Frank popped up behind Lenny.

"Lenny," he said with an air of concern that immediately gave me pause. "I need to borrow Harper for a minute."

Behind Frank, Meredith Hudson stood in her police uniform and bouncy blonde ponytail, talking quietly with Quinn. Before her, Quinn had her arms on her hips and was poking at the taller woman's chest aggressively.

"What's going on?" I asked Frank.

Without answering me, Frank swept an arm to the side. "We'll give you a call as soon as the Jeep is ready," he said pointedly.

"Of course, of course," Lenny stammered, pushing my phone at me and practically backing toward the door, his eyes wide.

Frank ushered us all toward the front of the shop. Lenny stumbled out the door while I turned to Meredith, taking a deep breath to steady my nerves. Quinn's face had two bright spots of color high on her cheeks and Meredith's mouth was bracketed in lines of tension.

"What's going on?" I asked, proud that my voice didn't waiver.

Meredith opened her mouth, but Quinn cut her off. "Derek's gone on a rampage," she announced. "He's smashing up the town."

My blood ran cold. "What?"

Sighing, Meredith started over. "The good news is that it looks like Mr. Dufort has left town."

"Left a path of destruction in his wake, is more like it," Quinn interjected, folding her arms across her chest.

Meredith mumbled something that sounded like "takes one to know one" under her breath before continuing. "This morning we got a call from the Bakers, who rent out their garage apartment during the convention every year." She shook her head. "When they went to clean the unit this morning, it was trashed. I showed them the picture of Dufort and they identified him as the man who rented it."

"Trashed?" I echoed numbly.

Meredith shrugged. "Tables overturned, dishes broken. That kind of stuff."

"He totally hulked out in there," Quinn said knowingly.

"Yeah, that's basically what it looked like," Meredith agreed reluctantly. "He even tore the curtains from the windows. Mrs. Baker is *pissed*." She drew out the word. "The other good news is that she's filed a report, which means if Dufort does come back to town, we have cause to pick him up immediately."

"Wow." I sagged, the tension finally easing from my shoulders. "I'm really sorry about the damage to her apartment, but that is good news."

"Yeah, the Chief wanted you to know," Meredith confirmed. "But he'd still like you to be careful, okay?"

"Okay," I agreed, tears pricking the corners of my eyes. "Please tell him thank you."

Frank walked Meredith out the door then disappeared into his office, his gaze studiously avoiding my emotional meltdown.

Quinn grabbed my hands and held on tight while I focused on taking deep, even breaths.

"You're okay," she told me firmly.

"Yup," I agreed, ignoring the thickness of my voice.

"Hey," she said, forcing my gaze to meet hers. "Your crazy ex has ridden his black horse over the horizon and you've got a naked hottie waiting for you at home. Life is pretty damn good."

I took a deep breath, a smile blossoming across my face. "It is, isn't it?"

Twelve

Ronan

I paced the living room, my bare feet slapping against the hardwood floor as I checked the clock for the thirteenth time in ten minutes. Harper was late. The shadows stretched longer across the walls, and the golden afternoon light had dimmed to a muted amber glow that did nothing to calm my restless energy.

"She's fine," I muttered to myself, running a hand through my hair. "Just running late. That's all."

But what if it wasn't? What if Derek—

Stop it. Harper's a grown woman who can handle herself.

Still, my eyes darted to the clock again. Twenty minutes late now.

I'd been human for hours now, watching the world through windows that might as well have been prison bars. The tiny cottage had seemed cozy in the night with Harper curled against me. Now the walls pressed in, suffocating me with each circuit of the living room.

The backyard called to me—just a few steps through the kitchen door. Green grass, fresh air, and Harper's garage where she kept her father's old Beetle. I'd helped her work on it the other night, our hands bumping into each other as we tinkered side by side.

"What's the worst that could happen?" I asked myself.

My mind played an image of a stuffed bear, lying inanimate on the wet grass, being eviscerated by a flock of birds. I stopped at the rear window and stared at the garage—so close, twenty yards at most. Could I make it?

"You used to be so much braver than this," I told my dim reflection in the glass.

Are we really doing this? Bruno had asked me when we'd pulled up to the bank that day.

Damn straight we are, I'd replied.

I'd had so much more confidence in our dream than the bank had. Turned out, the bank had been right. I'd been beating myself up for that mistake for fifty years.

But I wouldn't be here today, with Harper, if I hadn't taken a risk for my dream.

I scrawled a quick note onto the back of a napkin on the table and walked to the back door, heart hammering against my ribs. Through the glass, twenty yards of moonlit grass separated me from the garage. Twenty yards where anything could happen.

"Sometimes you have to take the risk," I said to myself, and opened the door.

Harper

I pushed open the front door, the weight of the day sloughing off my shoulders as I stepped into my sanctuary.

"Ronan?" I called, taking in the empty spot on the couch where I'd left the bear this morning. "Are you—you?"

The silence that answered sent a chill down my spine. My heartbeat quickened as I scanned the room.

"Hello?" I tried again, moving toward the bedroom.

That's when I spotted the napkin on the kitchen table, a messy scrawl across its surface. I snatched it up.

> *In the garage*
> —R

I blinked at the note, a grin spreading across my face. He'd gone outside? Brave man. Or extremely stupid man. The jury was still out.

I glanced out the kitchen window. Twilight had descended, painting the backyard in shades of purple and blue. Warm light glowed through the garage window, a beacon in the gathering darkness. It drew me out the back door and the evening air kissed my skin, cool and fresh after a day spent immersed in exhaust fumes and anxiety.

I pressed my palm against the garage door and paused. A deep voice hummed a tune I didn't recognize—something old and bluesy that made my toes curl.

I pushed the door open and there he stood. Ronan had his back to me, shoulders hunched over the open hood of Junebug. The sweatpants I'd given him hung low on his hips and the lean muscle of his back rose and lengthened as he leaned deeper into the engine compartment.

My breath caught in my throat, and I froze in the doorway, drinking in the sight of him.

"Hand me that 3/4 ratchet, would you, sweetheart?" Ronan asked without turning around, his voice rumbling through the small space.

"How'd you know it was me?" I asked, moving toward the workbench to grab the tool.

"Your footsteps." He straightened, wiping his hands on a shop rag as he turned to face me. "Light, but purposeful. Like you know exactly where you're going but you're not in any hurry to get there."

"Wow," I deadpanned, handing him the ratchet. "That's quite the pickup line."

His eyes crinkled at the corners. "Is it working?"

"Like a charm." I stepped closer, inhaling the intoxicating mix of motor oil, metal, and man.

He set the ratchet down and reached for my hand, his fingers warm and calloused against mine. Our lips met and the world fell away. The garage disappeared and the only thing that existed was Ronan's touch where it burned against me. Those lips, his fingers, the silken skin of his waist under my hand.

After a long, sweet moment we broke apart on a sigh and I stared at our joined hands, unable to meet his eyes. "Weren't you worried about coming out here? What if you would have changed outside?"

"I was terrified," he admitted with a soft laugh. "But sometimes you've got to take the risk." He tugged me closer. "Besides, I wanted to do something for you. Something real."

"You've done plenty of real things for me," I said, waggling my eyebrows.

Ronan's answering smile didn't quite meet his eyes. He ran his free hand over Junebug's fender. "I know what it's like to pour your soul into a machine. To see something broken and know in your gut that you can fix it, even when everyone else says it's a lost cause."

"Is that what happened with your garage?" I asked softly. "Frank mentioned some guy named Benny?"

Ronan's jaw tightened. "Yeah. We were young, stupid, and in way over our heads. I convinced the guys we could make it work." His laugh held no humor. "Turns out, running a business is harder than building engines."

"So what happened?" I leaned against Junebug, the cool metal of her fender seeping through my jeans.

"We needed money." Ronan released my hand and turned back to the engine, his shoulders tense. "The bank turned us down, so I went to Benny, the local loan shark. Bad idea."

"The worst," I agreed. "Frank said he was a bad guy."

"Frank knew Benny?" Ronan looked surprised.

"He said no one really believed you guys burned down Johnson's Garage. He mentioned Benny." I searched the dark green depths of Ronan's eyes. "Was he involved in the fire?"

Ronan's knuckles whitened as he gripped the edge of the hood. "We fell behind on payments. Benny suggested we 'remove the competition' by burning down Johnson's Garage." He shook his head. "I told him to go to hell."

"Good for you." I laid my hand over his.

"Not really." Ronan's voice dropped so low I had to strain to hear him. "He took Sean to 'motivate' me."

Ice slid down my spine. "He kidnapped your brother?"

"I found Sean's bike on the pier and I knew Benny had taken him. We ran to the garage." Ronan's gaze went distant. "But when we got there, Benny had already set it on fire with Sean inside."

"Oh, Ronan."

He nodded grimly. "I ran straight into the flames to get Sean out. That's the last thing I remember before..." He raised his arm, gesturing generally in the direction of the boardwalk.

My heart squeezed painfully in my chest. "And you think the others—your friends and Sean—they're also. ..?"

"I hope so. Better than the alternative."

I crossed the distance between us and wrapped my arms around his waist, pressing my cheek against his bare chest. His heartbeat thundered beneath my ear, strong and steady.

Ronan's arms came around me, pulling me tight against him. He buried his face in my hair, his breath warming my scalp.

"Thank you," he whispered. "For giving me a chance."

"Well, I did throw a wrench at your head." I tilted my head back to look at him, a smile tugging at my lips. "Besides, you're way hotter than my last boyfriend. Even with the occasional fur."

The tension in Ronan's face broke, replaced by a slow, dangerous smile that liquefied my insides. "Is that right?"

"Mmhmm." I trailed my fingers up his bare chest, feeling the muscles beneath jump at my touch. "Though I have to say, I'm a fan of this particular form."

"Are you now?" His voice dropped to a growl as his hands slid down to cup my ass. "You're playing with fire, sweetheart." With a swift movement that stole my breath, Ronan hoisted me up and deposited me onto the workbench, tools clattering to the floor.

"Harper Brinkman," he said, his voice rough as he pushed my knees apart and stepped between them, "you're going to be the death of me."

"What a way to go though, right?" I wrapped my legs around his waist, pulling him closer.

His mouth crashed down on mine, hot and demanding. I opened for him immediately, my fingers tangling in his hair as his tongue swept inside. He tasted like coffee and mint and something uniquely Ronan that made my head spin and my body melt.

His hands slid under my shirt, calloused palms scraping deliciously against my skin as they moved higher, leaving trails of fire in their wake. When he reached my breasts, I arched into his touch, moaning into his mouth.

"God, I've missed you," he murmured against my lips, thumbs brushing over my nipples.

"It's only been a day," I gasped, my hips rocking forward involuntarily.

"Too long." He tugged my shirt over my head, tossing it carelessly aside. "Way too long."

My bra followed quickly, and then Ronan's mouth was on my breast, hot and wet and perfect. I clutched at his shoulders, my head falling back as pleasure rocketed through me. The cool air of the garage pebbled my exposed skin into goosebumps—or maybe that was just Ronan's effect.

"Please," I begged, not entirely sure what I was asking for.

But Ronan seemed to know. His hands made quick work of my jeans, yanking them down along with my underwear as I lifted my hips to help. The workbench was cold and hard beneath my bare ass, but I couldn't have cared less as Ronan pushed his borrowed sweatpants down just enough to free himself.

"Is this okay?" he asked on a groan, stopping just short of where I needed him.

"Very okay." I watched through heavy-lidded eyes as he pushed toward me, into me. "Extremely okay. The most okay thing that ever—"

My babbling cut off with a gasp as he hit the spot inside me with his slow, deliberate thrust. My legs tightened around his waist as he filled me completely, stretching and satisfying in ways that made my toes curl.

"Still okay?" he asked, his forehead pressed against mine, breath coming in short pants.

"Yes, yes," I gasped, digging my heels into his lower back. "Move, Ronan. Please."

He did. With his hands gripping my hips, Ronan set a punishing pace that had the workbench creaking ominously beneath us. Each thrust hit something deep inside that made stars explode behind my eyelids. I clung to his shoulders, our bodies slick with sweat as we moved together in frantic harmony.

"Harper," he ground out, his rhythm faltering. "I'm going to—"

"Me too," I gasped, feeling the tension coiling tighter in my belly. "Don't stop."

Ronan slid one hand between us, his thumb finding my clit, and I shattered. Waves of pleasure crashed over me, each one lifting me higher than the last as I cried out his name. Ronan followed moments later, his body going rigid against mine as he groaned into my neck.

For a long moment, we stayed frozen, our ragged breathing the only sound in the garage. Ronan's weight pressed me into the workbench, but I couldn't have moved if I wanted to—my bones had turned to jelly.

"Holy hell," I finally managed, my voice barely above a whisper.

Ronan lifted his head, a satisfied smile spreading across his face. "Worth the risk of me turning back into a bear mid-stroke?"

I snorted, then dissolved into giggles that had him slipping out of me with a wince. "That would've been quite the experience."

"For both of us." He tucked himself away and pulled up his sweatpants before helping me down from the workbench on wobbly legs. "I have a feeling once you go bear, you never go back."

I smacked his chest. "That's terrible."

"But you laughed." He bent to retrieve my clothes, handing them over with exaggerated gallantry.

"I did not." I yanked on my jeans, the denim scraping over my sensitive skin. "I was choking on garage dust."

"Sure, sweetheart." Ronan's smile was infuriatingly smug. "Whatever helps you sleep at night."

I stuck my tongue out at him as I pulled my shirt back on, wincing as I caught a whiff of myself. "I need a shower."

"Allow me." Before I could protest, Ronan swept me into his arms, cradling me against his chest like I weighed nothing.

"Ronan!" I yelped, my arms automatically going around his neck. "Put me down!"

"Nope." He nudged the garage door open with his foot and carried me into the twilight. "I'm being chivalrous."

"You're being ridiculous." But I couldn't help the smile that spread across my face as he carried me across the yard. "What if you change back? You'll drop me on my ass."

"Then I'll have dropped the most beautiful ass in Santa Paola in fifty years," he said solemnly. "And that would be a real tragedy."

I laughed, pressing my face into his neck. "You're impossible."

"Yet here you are," he pointed out, nudging open the back door with his hip, "taking the risk with me."

"Yeah," I agreed softly as he carried me into our home. "I guess I am."

Thirteen

"You know what I want to know?" Quinn said, twirling on a stool in concentric half-circles as she addressed the teddy bear propped up on my workbench. "Where does his *equipment* go when he's a bear?"

"Quinn!" I hissed, slapping a hand over her mouth as I looked around wildly to make sure Frank was in his office. "What is wrong with you?"

She licked my palm. I yanked my hand away with a disgusted noise.

"What?" she asked innocently, batting her eyelashes.

"I will murder you with this socket wrench." I brandished the tool, my face on fire. "Right here in front of witnesses."

"What witnesses?" Quinn grinned, gesturing around the empty garage. "It's just us and the bear. And I don't think stuffed animals can testify in court."

I glanced at Ronan, his green glass eyes gleaming in the overhead fluorescents. The permanent smile stitched onto his face seemed just a bit smugger than usual.

"You're embarrassing him," I grumbled, burying my head back into the engine I was working on.

"Please." Quinn rolled her eyes.

I groaned, refusing to surface. "Why are we friends again?"

"Because I'm delightful." Quinn spun her chair again, the metal squeaking in protest. "Also, I'm the only one who knows your boyfriend is sometimes a bear, and I haven't sold the story to the National Enquirer yet, so you owe me."

"I hate that this is a valid point," I muttered.

The bell above the door jingled, and I straightened up as Lenny shuffled into the garage. His gaze moved around the space, sweeping over the mostly empty bay.

"Hi, Lenny," I called, pushing my chair away from the desk. "Your Jeep's all ready. Quinn has your invoice." I gave her a nudge and Quinn reluctantly stood and met Lenny at her desk.

"That's great," he mumbled, handing Quinn a credit card. While she ran the charge, he cleared his throat. "So, uh, Harper, how long have you been in Santa Paola?"

"Almost three months," I said, wiping my hands on a rag.

Lenny nodded, looking intently down at Quinn's desk. "And you moved here because you knew Quinn from college, right?"

I glanced over at Quinn, who gave me a silent shrug. "Yup, that's right," I answered slowly. "Everything okay?"

"Of course, of course!" Lenny gave a strangled laugh. "Just wondering about your, uh, background. Professional background! Like, did you always want to be a mechanic? Or did something inspire you?"

Behind us, Quinn's chair squeaked as she leaned forward, unabashedly eavesdropping.

"I grew up working on cars with my dad," I said cautiously. "Did my engineering degree but realized I preferred working with my hands. Why the sudden interest in my life story?"

Lenny's face flushed red. "No reason! Just curious. About you. Generally. As a person." He backed toward the door, fumbling in his pocket. "Actually, I just remembered I have to be somewhere."

I shared a bewildered look with Quinn, who shrugged dramatically.

"Thanks!" His voice cracked. "Great job on the Jeep. You're very talented. With cars, I mean. Mechanically. Very skilled with, uh, mechanical things."

"Thanks?"

"Okay, bye!" And with that, Lenny bolted from the garage like he had a pack of wolves on his heels.

The bell jangled violently as the door slammed shut behind him.

"What," Quinn asked into the silence that followed, "the actual hell was that?"

"I have no idea." I stared at the door, my brow furrowed. "That was kind of weird, even for Lenny, right?"

"Super weird." Quinn jumped up and leaned her elbows onto my workbench and pushed her face close to the bear's. "What do you think, Ronan? Any insights from the stuffed toy perspective?"

"He probably just had somewhere to be," I said, not entirely convinced. "Or maybe he's just being socially awkward. It's Lenny."

"Mmm, no. That was beyond regular Lenny awkwardness." Quinn poked Ronan's stomach. "What do you think, big guy?"

"Please don't assult my boyfriend," I said firmly, rescuing Ronan from Quinn's poking finger. Then I froze, staring at Quinn with stricken eyes.

Quinn's eyebrows shot up. "Boyfriend?"

"I mean, um..." I trailed off, remembering everything we'd done in my garage last night. The memory sent heat spiraling through my belly.

"Oh my god, you're in love with him," Quinn gasped, clapping her hands together delightedly. "You've gone and fallen for the cursed beefcake!"

"It's only been a couple of days," I protested, the denial automatic and hollow even to my own ears. "I barely know him."

"Honey, you're carrying his stuffed form around like a security blanket. You've practically moved him into your house. You're getting laid on the regular by a man who occasionally turns into a children's toy." Quinn ticked off each point on her fingers. "If that's not love, I don't know what is."

Was she right? The thought sent a jolt of panic through me. I glanced down at the bear's stitched smile, trying to imagine what expression the real Ronan would be wearing as he listened to this insane conversation. Was he be smirking? Horrified? Did he feel...whatever this was...too?

"I'm just helping him figure out his curse," I said finally. "It's...compassion."

"Is that what the kids are calling it these days?" Quinn laughed. "Well, compassion sure looks good on you. You're positively glowing."

I shoved Ronan into my messenger bag, careful to position him so his head poked out the top. "Speaking of the curse, I'm going to take him back to the boardwalk after work. See if there are any clues where I found him."

Quinn's expression softened. "Want me to come with you? Two sets of eyes are better than one."

"Thanks, but I'm not really alone." I lifted the bag to my shoulder, Ronan's fuzzy head bobbing with the movement. "Maybe having just him and me there will trigger something."

Quinn waggled her eyebrows again. "Trigger something, huh?"

"Not like that!" I swatted at her arm. "You have a one-track mind, you know that?"

"I contain multitudes," Quinn said sagely, spinning her chair back toward her computer. "Call me if you find anything. Or if your hot naked man makes an appearance. I'm dying to meet the human version of Mr. Cuddles."

The nickname had me rolling my eyes as I gathered my things. "I'll call you either way. And for the love of god, stop calling him Mr. Cuddles. It's embarrassing."

"For you or for him?" Quinn grinned.

"Both." I headed for the door, the bear's head peeking out of my bag. "See you tomorrow."

As the door closed behind me, Quinn called out, "Bye, Mr. Cuddles! Don't do anything I wouldn't do!"

The breeze off the afternoon's rough seas tangled my hair as I trudged along the boardwalk, my messenger bag bumping against my hip with each step. The setting sun cast long shadows across weathered planks, and the distant crash of waves provided a soothing backdrop to my one-sided conversation.

"So this is where it all began," I said to the bear poking out of my bag. I lowered my voice as I passed an elderly couple. "This is definitely not normal behavior."

There were few locals strolling along the weathered planks, and the boardwalk stretched before me, oddly peaceful without the summer crowds. Salt mingled with hints of cotton candy and fried dough in the air—phantom smells from summers past that never quite faded.

Most of the shops along the boardwalk were shuttered for the season, but the neon sign above the arcade flickered halfheartedly against the darkening sky. My heart rate kicked up a notch.

"This is it," I whispered to Ronan, moving to the left side of the building where two large, dark shadows sat beneath a low awning.

The lights from the promenade didn't reach here, so I pulled out my phone to use as a flashlight. The glow bounced off the glass of the claw machine and I gasped.

It was full of bears. And they all looked just like Ronan.

"Hot damn," I breathed, pressing my face against the glass. I counted. And counted again, realization dawning.

There were five more bears.

I fumbled Ronan out of my messenger bag, holding him up to the glass. "Look, Ronan! It's them." I swallowed, my heart pounding. "I think it's them."

There were variations, but each bear had the same vintage style, with jointed limbs and bright glass eyes.

Different colors, different fur, but unmistakably part of a set.

"We need to get them out of there," I whispered, digging in my pocket for quarters. I came up empty and let the strap of my bag fall down my arm to dig inside. "I know I have quarters in here," I said, my voice rising with an edge of desperation. I crouched down, leaning Ronan carefully against the claw machine, and opened my bag onto the ground. "Come on, man!"

"Talking to stuffed animals now, Harper? That's a new low, even for you."

The voice slithered up my spine like ice water and I froze.

Not Derek. Not now.

I stood and turned slowly, my heartbeat thundering in my ears.

He stood between me and the boardwalk, his face in shadow and his body outlined by the lights behind him.

"Surprise," he said, spreading his arms wide. "Did you miss me?"

"No," I replied flatly.

The faint gleam of Derek's smile disappeared. "You always were too clever for your own good."

He stepped closer, and I backed up, stumbling over my bag.

"What do you want, Derek?" I bit out.

"What do I want?" Derek repeated, his voice softening dangerously. "I want you to stop this childish tantrum and come home."

Home. The word tasted like ash in my mouth. "This is my home now. I'm not going anywhere."

"This dump?" Derek's laugh scraped across my nerves. "Please. You don't belong here, with these people." He spat out the last word like it was poison. "You belong with me, Harper. You're mine."

"I don't belong to anyone." I straightened my spine. "You're the one who doesn't belong here. You need to leave, Derek."

"I'm not going anywhere without you," Derek hissed, his perfect facade cracking to reveal the monster beneath. His hand whipped out and latched onto my jaw, tilting my face toward his as he stepped closer. "I loved you, you stupid bitch."

"You never loved me," I spat, struggling against his hold.

His expression darkened. "Don't tell me how I feel!"

The hand on my face squeezed until tears sprang to my eyes. My hands clawed at his arm, nails digging in, but he just spun me around. Now the light from the boardwalk was falling onto his face and my blood ran cold at the madness in his eyes.

"You think you can just walk away from what we had? Start over in some stupid little podunk town?" His fingers tightened, and stars danced at the edges of my vision. "There is no starting over, Harper. There's only me."

A strangled sound escaped my throat as I fought for air. My lungs burned. The adrenaline coursing through my veins had nowhere to go, no outlet against his superior strength.

This was it. After all my careful planning, all my new beginnings, Derek had found me. And this time—

"Let. Her. Go."

The voice—deep, dangerous, and achingly familiar—cut through the haze of my panic like a blade. Derek's grip slackened in surprise, and I sucked in a desperate breath.

Standing behind Derek, naked as the day he was born, was Ronan. Six feet of tattooed muscle and righteous fury.

"Who the hell—" Derek began, turning toward the voice.

He never finished the sentence. Ronan's fist connected with Derek's face with a sickening crack, sending him staggering backward. Released, I slumped to the boardwalk, gasping for air.

"You must be Derek," Ronan said conversationally, as if he weren't standing completely naked in a public arcade with the other man's blood on his knuckles. "I've been looking forward to meeting you."

Derek clasped a hand over his split lip, eyes wide as he took in the naked man before him. "Who the hell are you?"

"I'm the guy who's going to rearrange your teeth if you don't walk away right now," Ronan replied, baring his teeth in a feral smile.

The three of us were frozen in a bizarre tableau—Derek with his perfectly pressed polo now rumpled and spotted with his own blood, Ronan gloriously naked and battle-ready, and me sprawled at their feet.

The unmistakable wail of a police siren cut through the silence and flashing lights painted the boardwalk in lengths of blue and red.

Derek's face contorted with rage and he sprinted down the boardwalk, away from the approaching crunch of tires over weathered boards.

I turned to Ronan, relief flooding through me. "Are you okay? We need to—"

The words died in my throat. Where Ronan had stood just seconds before, there was nothing but empty space. My gaze dropped to the ground, where a familiar teddy bear now lay in a circle of light from the approaching cruiser.

"Harper?" Meredith jumped out of her vehicle, blonde ponytail swinging as her head turned from side to side, hand hovering over her holstered weapon. "Are you alright? We got a report of an altercation."

I clutched the bear to my chest, heart hammering. "I'm fine," I managed, hoping my voice didn't betray the adrenaline still surging through my system. "I'm okay."

Meredith's eyes narrowed at me where I crouched on the ground, wild-eyed and disheveled, clutching a teddy bear like a lifeline.

"You don't look fine." She knelt down beside me, resting a gentle hand on my shoulder. "What happened?"

Tears pricked at the corners of my eyes and the words were stuck in my throat. When a figure emerged from the shadows to my right, I nearly jumped out of my skin.

Meredith reached for her weapon. "Who's there?" she demanded forcefully.

"It's me, Lenny Burnstein. I'm the one who called 911." Lenny stepped closer, his hands raised and his eyes darting nervously between us.

"Harper, are you okay?" he asked, his voice pitched higher than normal. "I saw that guy attack you."

Meredith turned to him, frown deepening. "What guy?"

"He took off down the boardwalk." Lenny's gaze flicked to me, then to the teddy bear in my arms, then back to Meredith. "Did you know that guy, Harper?"

I swallowed, finding my voice again. "It was my ex-boyfriend, Derek Dufort. He was trying to get me to go with him."

Lenny turned back to Meredith. "I saw the whole thing, Officer Hudson. He grabbed her face and knocked her down."

Meredith sat back on her heels, shaking her head. "Shit. That's attempted kidnapping." She looked at me more closely. "Are you sure you're not injured? Can you stand up?"

I nodded and the two of them helped me to my feet before Meredith went back to her car to make a call. Left alone, Lenny and I locked eyes. An unspoken acknowledgment passed between us.

Fourteen

The rain started falling as Meredith's patrol car pulled up to my cottage.

"You sure you don't want me to call Quinn?" she asked for the third time, her eyes flicking to the teddy bear clutched against my chest. "I really don't like the idea of you being alone tonight."

"I'm not..." I caught myself and cleared my throat. "I'll be fine. I've upgraded all the locks, and Derek has no idea where I live." I hoped. "Besides, it's after midnight. Quinn needs her full eight hours or she gets cranky."

Meredith's mouth twitched. "Isn't she always?"

I paused before opening the door, clutching the bear to my chest. "Thanks for everything, Meredith. I mean it."

She nodded, her ponytail bobbing in the dim light. "Just doing my job. We'll find him, Harper."

"I know you will." I didn't sound convinced, even to myself.

I lurched out of the car and hurried up the path to my front door, my shoes squishing in the sudden mud. Once I had the door unlocked I turned to wave at Meredith and then closed it firmly behind me. I turned the lock in the knob and set the new deadbolt, then turned and leaned against the door, exhaling a breath I'd been holding for hours.

Ronan remained stubbornly inanimate in my arms, so I kicked off my muddy shoes and padded through the living room and straight into my bedroom. Leaving him in the middle of the bed, I walked like a zombie into my bathroom, shedding clothing along the way.

Hot water sluiced over my skin, washing away the grime of the evening and easing the knot of tension between my shoulder blades. My jaw was tender as I scrubbed at my skin, scouring away the top layer. Any epithelial cells that Derek had come into contact with went down the drain, washed away by the scalding hot water.

I wasn't even aware that I was sobbing until a large, male hand wrapped around my shoulder.

Not Derek.

Ronan turned me toward him and gently pulled me into his arms and I clung to his solid, real body as I let go of my fear.

When the water finally began to cool, I reluctantly pulled away and looked up at the man holding me with a sheepish grin. "Sorry," I shrugged. "Not sure where that came from."

I turned off the water and Ronan pulled me back into his arms.

"You have nothing to be sorry for, sweetheart," he told me, his eyes a clear, dark green that pierced right into my soul for a moment before they closed and he pulled me into his body. "I should have been able to protect you better," he murmured into my damp hair.

I pulled back just enough to look up at him. "Are you kidding me? You were amazing. You punched Derek in the face! Naked!"

A ghost of a smile crossed his lips. "Not my finest moment, strategically speaking."

"It was pretty spectacular from where I was sitting," I assured him, rising on tiptoes to press a kiss to the corner of his mouth. "My knight in shining...nothing."

That earned me a real smile, though it faded quickly. "I was so scared, Harper. When I saw him hurting you..."

"I know." I stroked my thumb along his cheekbone. "But I'm okay now. We're okay."

We stood like that for a long moment, the tapping of the rain on the old roof providing a soothing backdrop to our breathing. Finally, Ronan's eyes opened, focused and intent.

"Lenny saw me," he said quietly.

I nodded. "I think so, yeah. He was acting weird at the garage earlier today, too. I don't think he just happened to be walking by."

Ronan ran a hand through his hair. "No, I don't think so either." He trailed off, his gaze drifting back to the window.

"What is it?" I prompted.

"The claw machine," he said, his voice tight. "Harper, there were five more bears in there."

"I know." I squeezed his hands. "Do you think it's them?"

"It has to be." His voice cracked on the word. "They've been trapped in that damn machine for fifty years, just like me."

"We'll get them out," I promised. "First thing tomorrow, I'll go back with a roll of quarters and—"

"What if it doesn't work?" Ronan broke off, shaking his head. "What if they can't shift and they're stuck like that forever?"

I stepped closer, my wet body pressing into his. "Ronan, look at me." I waited until his green eyes met mine. "We're going to figure this out. Together."

He searched my face, desperation warring with hope in his eyes. "Together?"

"Together. Because I love you," I blurted out.

The words hung in the air between us, as tangible as the rain against the windows. My cheeks burned, but I didn't look away.

Ronan's expression softened, the tension melting from his shoulders. "Harper Brinkman," he said, his voice a low rumble that vibrated through me, "you are the most extraordinary woman I have ever met."

"Is that a good thing or a bad thing?" I asked, only half-joking.

"It's everything." He reached for me, his hands cupping my face with exquisite gentleness. "Did you see the fortune teller machine on the boardwalk?"

I nodded my head, unable to speak past the lump in my throat.

"That night, before we found Sean in Johnson's Garage—before I knew that Benny had taken Sean—I was walking on the boardwalk and I saw the fortune teller." He shook his head, his gaze far away. "I'd walked that boardwalk a thousand times, but I'd never seen it there before. There was a coin sitting on the boardwalk right in front of it and I was putting it into the machine before I knew what I was doing."

My mouth opened, ready to point out how similar his story was to the night I'd found him, but something held me back.

"The lights came on and the fortune teller asked me for my wish." Ronan's gaze sharpened and I knew he was seeing me again. "I wished for my brother and my friends to find true happiness in their lives." His thumbs stroked my cheekbones. "I'd screwed up with the garage, with the loan from Benny. I didn't think I deserved it, but I wanted it for them."

"Ronan—"

"But now I know," he continued, his eyes never leaving mine. "You're my happiness, Harper. You're the reason I'm here. And I love you more than I thought possible."

My breath caught in my throat. "Even though I'm always covered in grease and tried to kill you with a wrench?"

His laugh warmed me from the inside out. "Especially because of those things."

"Good," I whispered. "Because I love you, too."

His expression turned serious. "Whatever happens with the curse, with my friends, with your ex...I'm in this. All the way. For as long as you'll have me."

"Even if it's forever?" I asked, my voice small.

"Especially if it's forever." The corner of his mouth ticked up. "I've waited fifty years for you, Harper Brinkman. I'm not going anywhere."

"Promise?" I hated how vulnerable I sounded, but I couldn't help it.

"I promise." He sealed the vow with another kiss, this one deeper, more insistent.

My arms wound around his neck as I melted into him, the last of my defenses crumbling. His hands slid down my sides to grip my hips, pulling me flush against him. The heat of his skin warmed mine where we connected, and I gasped as his tongue swept into my mouth.

With a growl that vibrated through his chest and into mine, Ronan lifted me off my feet. My legs wrapped around his waist instinctively as he carried me to the bedroom, our lips never breaking contact.

The bedsprings creaked as he laid me down, his body following mine onto the mattress. Outside, thunder rumbled, punctuating the rhythm of the rain.

"I love you," I whispered against his lips, the words no longer frightening.

Ronan's smile was radiant in the dim light. "Say it again."

"I love you," I repeated, louder this time. "I love you, Ronan O'Neill, even when you're small and fuzzy."

"Especially when I'm small and fuzzy," he corrected, nipping at my lower lip.

"Mmm, I don't know about that," I murmured, running my hands down his chest to explore areas further south. "The human version has certain...advantages."

His laugh rumbled through both of us. "Is that so?"

"Definite anatomical advantages," I confirmed, giving a firm squeeze to demonstrate my point.

Ronan's breath hitched. "You make a compelling argument."

"I'm very persuasive."

"The most persuasive," he agreed, his voice strained. "Harper—"

Whatever he was about to say dissolved into a groan as his head dropped to my shoulder, breath hot against my neck.

"You're killing me, sweetheart," he muttered, teeth grazing my earlobe.

"Not yet," I promised. "But the night is young."

With a swift movement that left me breathless, Ronan pinned my hands above my head, his body hovering over mine. "Two can play that game."

His calloused palm moved across the soft skin of my stomach. I arched into his touch, a whimper escaping my lips as his fingers brushed the underside of my breast.

"Please," I whispered, not entirely sure what I was asking for.

But Ronan seemed to know. He lowered his mouth to my breast and the wet heat of his tongue sent electricity shooting down my spine.

"You're so beautiful," he murmured against my skin. "Every inch of you."

He settled between my thighs, his weight supported on his forearms as he hovered above me. The first brush of him against me had me gasping, my legs wrapping around his waist to hold him close.

"I love you," Ronan said again, his eyes holding mine. "I need you to know that."

"I do know," I assured him, cupping his face. "I love you, too."

With that, he pushed forward, filling me in one long, slow thrust that had both of us moaning. For a moment, we stayed perfectly still, forehead to forehead, sharing breath and heartbeats.

"Okay?" he whispered.

"More than okay," I assured him, rocking my hips up to meet his. "Perfect."

Ronan began to move then, setting a rhythm that matched the storm outside—building slowly, inexorably, toward a crescendo. Each thrust drove me higher, the tension coiling tighter in my belly with every movement of his hips against mine.

"Ronan," I gasped as he hit a particularly sensitive spot. "Right there."

He adjusted his angle, hitting that same spot again and again until stars danced behind my eyelids. At some point he'd released my hands and now my nails dug into his shoulders, leaving half-moons in his skin that I'd apologize for later.

"Harper," he growled, his movements becoming more urgent. "I'm close."

"Me too," I panted, teetering on the edge. "Don't stop."

He slipped a hand between us, his thumb rubbing firmly across my clit, and I shattered. Waves of pleasure crashed over me, each one higher than the last as I cried out his name. Ronan followed moments later, his body going rigid against mine as he buried his face in my neck with a groan.

For a long moment, we lay tangled together, our hearts racing in tandem as we caught our breath. The rain had slowed to a gentle patter against the window, as if the storm had spent its fury alongside ours.

Ronan rolled to his side, bringing me with him so I was tucked against his chest. I traced idle patterns on his skin, savoring the way his muscles jumped beneath my fingertips.

"What are you thinking?" he asked, pressing a kiss to the top of my head.

"We're going to get them out, Ronan," I promised, propping myself up on his chest to look him in the eye. "Your brother, your friends. We'll find a way."

His smile was soft and a little sad. "I know we will. Together."

"Together," I agreed, leaning down to seal the vow with a kiss.

Fifteen

Insistent banging on my front door yanked me from sleep like a trout on a line. I groaned and burrowed deeper under the covers, pressing my face into Ronan's warm chest.

"Harper!" Quinn's voice pierced through my door along with her knocking. "Open up or I'm breaking in!"

"Make it stop," I mumbled into Ronan's skin and his chest rumbled with laughter beneath my cheek.

"Harper Elizabeth Brinkman!" Quinn's voice rose an octave. "I have coffee and a baseball bat, and I will use both of them!"

"Coffee?" My head popped up, suddenly interested.

Ronan laughed again, pressing a kiss to my forehead. "Your priorities are inspiring."

I ignored him and rolled out of bed as Quinn's banging intensified.

"Ten seconds before I start smashing windows!"

"She'll do it," I warned him, yanking a robe around my naked body and cinching it tight. "And I really like these windows."

Ronan looked torn between laughter and terror. "Harper—"

Too late. The sound of a key scraping in the lock echoed through the cottage.

"And she has a key," I hissed, yanking him bodily from the bed and shoving him toward the closet. "Hide!"

The front door burst open as I closed the closet door on Ronan's stunned face. I spun around, heart hammering in my chest, to find Quinn standing in my bedroom doorway with a baseball bat in one hand and a cardboard tray holding two large cups of coffee in the other.

"What. The. Hell," she said, each word punctuated with a step into the room. "Meredith called me at five a.m. Five! To tell me that Derek attacked you on the boardwalk last night and you didn't bother to call me?"

"I was going to tell you at work?" It came out as a question rather than the statement I'd intended.

Quinn's eyes narrowed. "You were attacked, Harper. By your psycho ex-boyfriend. Who has now assaulted you twice and seems to have developed a creepy stalker obsession with you."

"When you put it that way, it does sound pretty bad," I admitted.

"Ya think?" Quinn thrust the cardboard tray of coffees at me. "Here. I figured you'd need this to function today."

I accepted one of the cups, inhaling the rich scent of espresso. "You're an angel."

"I know." Quinn propped the bat against the wall and crossed her arms. "So, where is he?"

My heart skipped a beat. "Who?"

"Mr. Cuddles." Quinn rolled her eyes. "Meredith said you were clutching that teddy bear like a lifeline when she dropped you off."

Relief washed over me. "Oh, um, he's around here somewhere," I said vaguely, waving toward the living room.

"Mmm-hmm." Quinn didn't look convinced. "Well, hurry up and get dressed. I'm escorting you to work today."

"That's really not necessary—"

"I'm armed," Quinn pointed to the wooden weapon, "and caffeinated. I've got this."

I sighed, recognizing the steel in her voice. "Fine. Give me ten minutes."

"You have five." Quinn snatched the other cup from the tray and marched out of the room. "And tell your closet I said hi!" she called over her shoulder.

I waited until she was out of sight before opening the closet door. Instead of Ronan's tall, muscular form, a teddy bear sat on the floor amidst my shoes.

"Sorry about that," I whispered, trying not to laugh.

Exactly four minutes and thirty seconds later, I emerged from the bedroom fully dressed, with the bear tucked securely under my arm. Quinn sat at my kitchen table, scrolling through her phone with one hand while the other maintained a white-knuckled grip on the baseball bat.

She looked up as I entered. "Ready for work, Goldilocks?"

"As I'll ever be." I gestured to the door. "Lead on, Macduff!"

Outside the morning air was cool and damp from last night's rain. Quinn marched ahead of me, looking left and right like a particularly paranoid meerkat, the bat swinging dangerously with each movement.

"You're going to take someone's head off with that thing," I warned, clutching the bear tighter against my side.

"That's sort of the point," Quinn replied cheerfully as we piled into her car.

"I can't believe I'm letting you drive me to work," I muttered as I buckled myself in. "I'd probably be safer walking."

Quinn waved a hand at me dismissively and started the car. "That mailbox came out of nowhere and you know it."

"It was stationary," I pointed out. "As mailboxes tend to be."

Quinn huffed. "You're so judgmental." She took a sip of her coffee, side-eyeing the bear nestled between us. "So, did boytoy make an appearance last night? After Meredith scared Derek away?"

"Actually, Ronan did a pretty good job of scaring Derek before Meredith arrived."

Quinn braked a little too hard and whipped her head around to stare at me in indignation. "DD got to meet Naked Hot Guy before I did? No fair!"

I shrugged and braced myself. This was going to add insult to injury. "And I think Lenny saw him, too," I told her apologetically.

"Oh, man," Quinn groused.

I patted her shoulder as she turned onto Main Street. "What really worries me is that I'm pretty sure Lenny actually saw Ronan shift."

Quinn's eyes got wide. "Holy crap," she gasped.

I nodded. "Indeed. Hopefully Lenny can keep a secret."

"Well, tell me you at least got lucky last night," she begged, pulling into the small parking lot beside the garage.

Heat crept up my neck. "I don't kiss and tell."

"That's a yes," Quinn crowed triumphantly. "I knew it! I'm going to need all of the details."

"Absolutely not!"

Quinn's laughter filled the car as shut off the engine. In front of us, the red brick facade of Johnson's Garage stood firm against the soft blue of the morning sky. Through the window I could see Frank moving around inside, setting up for the day. The familiar sights of the weathered sign and the oil-stained concrete settled something in my chest. This was my place now. My home. And no one, especially not Douchebag Derek, was going to take it from me.

"What's with the face?" Quinn asked as we climbed out of the car. She opened her back door to retrieve her trusty bat.

"What face?"

"That whole..." she waved her hand in front of my face as we walked toward the garage, "determined, badass, 'I'm-going-to-fix-this-carburetor-or-die-trying' expression."

I smiled, the tension in my shoulders easing slightly. "Just thinking that I'm not going to let Derek ruin this for me. Any of it." I glanced down at Ronan's fuzzy head poking out of my bag.

Quinn's expression softened. "Good. Because if he tries, I'll introduce his kneecaps to my little friend here." She patted the bat lovingly.

"You're kind of scary, you know that?"

"Damn straight."

By mid-morning, it became clear that Lenny could not, in fact, keep a secret.

Dan from the hardware store was the first to arrive, ostensibly to drop off some specialty screws Frank had ordered. But instead of just dropping off the package and heading back out, he lingered.

"Anything else, Dan?" Frank asked, as the other man stood awkwardly near my workbench.

Dan jumped, swinging back to Frank. He waved a hand toward where the teddy bear sat propped up among my tools. "Just admiring your new assistant there, Harper."

"Oh," I said blankly. "Um, thanks."

Quinn, who had been eavesdropping shamelessly from her desk, snorted into her coffee. I shot her a warning look.

Frank moved closer to my work station, inserting himself in Dan's line of sight. "We're all good here."

Dan's face fell slightly. "Of course, of course. I've got to get back to the shop." He scratched the back of his neck. "Just wanted to say—if you need anything, Harper..." His voice trailed off and he started again, more firmly. "This town takes care of its own, and you're one of us now."

Warmth bloomed in my chest. "Thanks, Dan."

After Dan left, the parade began in earnest.

"Can you blame them?" Quinn gestured widely. "Small towns run on gossip."

"Hello, dears." Mrs. Peterson glided into the garage in a cloud of perfume and hair spray.

"Mrs. Peterson!" Quinn jumped up to greet her. "What can we do for you today?"

"Oh, nothing for me, dear." Mrs. Peterson waved a ring-laden hand as she passed Quinn's desk. "I heard about Harper's troubles with that horrible man last night," she continued, making her way to my workbench. "I just wanted to pop in to offer my support."

I swallowed hard. "News travels fast."

"Doesn't it, though?" Mrs. Peterson's laugh tinkled like wind chimes. She reached out and, before I could stop her, picked up Ronan. "What a handsome young man," she cooed, turning him this way and that.

"Um, that's my..." I trailed off, unsure how to finish. Toy? My boyfriend?

"Emotional support animal," Quinn supplied helpfully.

Mrs. Peterson's eyes twinkled behind her glasses. "Is that what we're calling it these days?"

She set Ronan back on the bench with surprising gentleness, then leaned in close to me. "Everything will be okay," she whispered, her breath smelling faintly of peppermint and something spicier, like cinnamon. "Don't let that one go, dear. He's been waiting an awfully long time for you."

Before I could respond, she straightened up and adjusted her glasses. "Well, I must be off. Bingo waits for no woman."

And with that, she swept out of the garage as dramatically as she'd entered, leaving behind only the lingering scent of aquanet and a knot of anxiety in my stomach.

"Did that seem weird to you?" I asked Quinn once Mrs. Peterson was out of earshot.

"Weirder than usual, you mean?" Quinn shrugged.

I glanced at Ronan, wondering what he'd made of the encounter. His green glass eyes stared back, unreadable as always.

"Time for a break," Frank announced, wiping his hands on a rag as he emerged from beneath a Chevy. "Lunch at the diner is on me today, girls."

Quinn and I exchanged surprised looks.

"That's really nice of you, Frank, but—" I began.

"Chief Hudson said to keep an eye on you." Frank's tone brooked no argument. "So go wash up and we'll head out."

"Dad, seriously?" Quinn rolled her eyes. "Harper doesn't need a babysitter."

"Never said she did." Frank grabbed his jacket from the hook by the door. "But I need lunch, and possibly pie."

I hesitated, glancing at Ronan. I couldn't exactly leave him here, but carrying a teddy bear into the diner would definitely raise some eyebrows.

Frank followed my gaze. "You can bring the bear."

"I—what?"

"The bear." Frank nodded toward Ronan. "Bring him."

Silence followed Frank's words and I glanced at Quinn to find her mouth hanging open.

"Dad...?" Quinn started, letting the question trail off.

"This town may be full of busybodies, but they all have good intentions." Frank interrupted. "Harper's been through enough without having to worry about leaving her stuff unattended."

My throat tightened with unexpected emotion. "Thanks, Frank."

He grunted in response, already heading for the door. "Come on. Meat loaf waits for no man."

The brief walk to the diner was mercifully uneventful, though I couldn't shake the feeling of eyes on us from every storefront we passed as I clutched my bear-stuffed bag over my shoulder. Frank walked slightly ahead, his broad shoulders blocking most of my view, while Quinn stuck close to my side, baseball bat swinging at her side. I'd tried to talk her into leaving it at the garage to no avail.

"You know you can't bring that into the diner," I'd pointed out.

"Watch me," she'd muttered darkly.

The diner was bustling with the lunch crowd when we arrived, the bell on the door announcing our entrance with a cheerful jingle that belied the tension in my shoulders. Conversations paused momentarily as heads turned toward us, then resumed with slightly more animated gestures and whispers.

"Frank!" Agatha hurried over, her black combat boots squeaking against the linoleum. "I saved you guys a booth in the back."

"Thanks, Agatha," Frank said, as we followed her through the maze of tables.

Chief Hudson looked up from his newspaper as we walked by, coffee mug paused halfway to his mouth. "Frank," he acknowledged as a meaningful look passed between the older men. He gave me a nod and I waved back inanely and kept moving to the booth Agatha waved us into.

"I'd tell you to ditch the lumber, Quinn," the Chief said, as she shuffled past him with her bat, "but given the circumstances, I'll make an exception."

I pushed my bag across the bench, sliding in after it. Frank took the seat opposite me, with Quinn squeezing in beside him, the bat propped between her knees under the table.

Quinn preened. "See?" she hissed at me across the table. "Even the law is on my side."

"The Chief probably just doesn't want to argue with you," I muttered.

Cleo bustled over with menus and water glasses. "What can I get you three? Frank, the meatloaf special, I assume?"

"You know it." Frank barely glanced at the menu.

"I'll have a cheeseburger," Quinn decided. "Extra pickles."

"Chicken club for me, please. Extra fries," I added.

Cleo's eyes flicked to the bear's head peeking out from the top of my bag, a smile playing at the corners of her mouth. "And nothing for your little friend?"

Heat crept up my neck and I stared back at her dumbly.

Quinn leaned forward with an evil grin. "He's stuffed," she announced loud enough for the entire diner to hear.

"Lucky girl," Cleo said with a wink.

As she walked away with our orders, I buried my face in my hands. "This is so embarrassing."

"Nah, it's awesome," Quinn assured me. "Everyone's just glad you've got someone looking out for you, even if he is occasionally plush."

Frank cleared his throat. "So. You gonna tell me what's really going on with that bear?"

I choked on my water and froze, staring at Frank with wide eyes.

"What do you mean?" I asked, my voice squeaking slightly.

Frank leveled me with a look that said he wasn't buying my innocent act. "I've been around the block a few times,, Harper. I know when something's fishy. And that bear"—he nodded toward my bag—"smells like a whole can of tuna."

"Dad," Quinn hissed, "they're in love!"

"Quinn!" I kicked her under the table.

Frank's mustache twitched. "Is that right?"

"Kind of," I admitted, my shoulders slumping in defeat. "It's really complicated."

"Usually is." Frank took a sip of his water. "He fixed the Triumph, didn't he?"

I blinked. "How did you—"

"Nobody else in town could've done work that clean." Frank shrugged. "Plus, your wrench set was rearranged."

"You monitor my wrench positions?" I asked, incredulous.

Frank's eyes crinkled at the corners. "Whoever moved 'em knew what they were doing. Not too many people know Triumphs that well" He nodded firmly. "Especially that particular Triumph."

Quinn looked between us, mouth agape. "Wait, you know about Ronan?"

"Suspected." Frank's gaze shifted to the bear. "Hoped."

Before I could formulate a response, Cleo returned with our food, setting steaming plates before each of us.

"Your secret's safe with us, honey," she whispered as she placed my sandwich in front of me. "Some things in this town are better left unsaid."

I stared after her as she walked away and the Chief looked up from his paper and—I swear to god—winked at me. I considered having a heart attack right at that moment.

"This is really good meatloaf," Frank murmured into his plate, subject obviously closed.

Sixteen

"Everyone knows," I muttered to Quinn as we made our way back to the garage after lunch. "And no one is freaking out." I was still trying to process that information.

Frank grunted as he walked ahead of us. "Santa Paola is a tourist town. We've seen stranger things."

"Really?" I asked dubiously. "Like what?"

He glanced over his shoulder with an uncharacteristic twinkle in his eyes. "Quinn."

"Dad!" Quinn slapped Frank on the shoulder, laughing through her pretend outrage. She turned to me with a smile. "Seriously, though. This is the off season. Just wait until all of the wackos come flooding back next summer."

"Some never left," Frank murmured quietly under his breath and the three of us cracked up as we approached the garage.

Quinn huffed, pointing her bat at her father's back. "You're one to talk, Mr. I-Wear-The-Same-Blue-Shirt-Every-Day."

"It's a different blue shirt," Frank corrected, fishing in his pocket for his keys. "They just all look the same."

I laughed, the tension in my shoulders easing slightly with the familiar banter. "You two are ridiculous."

"He started it," Quinn muttered.

"You deserved it, sweetie," Frank replied, his voice gentler than his words as he reached for the doorknob. "You know—"

He stopped abruptly, the door open only inches, and shot his arm out to block our path.

"Girls, run back to the diner and get the Chief," he murmured, brow furrowing.

"What's wrong?" Quinn asked, stepping closer.

Frank frowned, pushing the door open wider. "Do as I say, Quinnie."

"Did you forget to lock the door when we left?" Quinn asked, ignoring Frank's gesture and moving up close behind him to peer through the cracked door.

A chill skittered down my spine and I fumbled my phone out of my back pocket. I'd entered the Chief's number into my contacts, so it only took me a second to bring it up on the screen.

"Wait here," Frank whispered, pushing the door open.

"Dad—" Quinn started, but Frank was already moving forward.

He stepped into the dim interior of the garage, his shoulders tense as he peered into the shadows. Everything seemed normal—tools in their places, cars waiting patiently for repair, Quinn's desk a chaotic explosion of paperwork.

"I don't see any—"

The blow came out of nowhere, a blur that connected against Frank's temple with a sickening crack. He crumpled to the concrete floor like a marionette with its strings cut.

"Dad!" Quinn cried out. She threw herself through the doorway and collapsed to the concrete floor beside his still body.

The phone fell from my numb fingers and I lurched after her. A form emerged from the shadows and every muscle in my body froze.

Not Derek. Please, not Derek.

"It's time to go home now, Harper," he stated calmly, as if we'd just been out for a nice little stroll. He looked crisp and cool in a perfectly ironed polo shirt and khakis. A drop of blood dripped from the tire iron he held by his side.

Between us, Quinn gently maneuvered Frank onto his back. She brushed the hair from his forehead to reveal a bloody gash above one eye.

"I've been incredibly patient, but this nonsense ends now," Derek continued.

Quinn looked up at him, a fiery rage in her eyes. "You son of a bitch," she growled, reaching for the bat lying at her side.

"Quinn, don't!" I shouted, dropping to my knees by her side to grab at her arm. My bag spilled onto the floor, Ronan tumbling onto the concrete.

Derek's eyes flicked to the bear, a sneer twisting his features. "Playing with stuffed toys now? I'm so disappointed in you, Harper."

"Leave us alone, Derek," I bit out. "Get out."

Quinn strained against my grip, her face contorted with rage. "I'm going to rip your—"

"Shut up." The venom in Derek's voice sliced through the air. "Both of you, shut up."

Frank groaned softly, a small puddle of blood forming beneath his head. The sight of it—dark red against the oil-stained concrete—sent a surge of anger through me that momentarily overpowered my fear.

"What do you want, Derek?" I demanded, pushing myself to my feet and stepping between him and Quinn.

"What do I want?" Derek repeated, his voice lilting with an almost sing-song quality that raised every hair on my body. "I want what's mine, Harper."

I shook my head in confusion. "What are you talking about? I don't have anything of yours."

"Do you really not get it?" Derek tilted his head at me, a frown forming between his perfectly arched brows.

"Get what?" I threw my hands up in exasperation. "I didn't take anything, Derek. Everything we bought together, every piece of furniture, our savings--I left it all."

He stared at me sadly, as if I'd failed some test.

"What?" I screamed at him. "What do you want?"

Derek took one step forward and I tensed. He was close enough now to reach out and grab me, but Frank and Quinn were on the floor behind me and there was nowhere to go.

"You," he said softly.

I waited for him to continue but the one word just hung in the air between us. Finally I asked, "Me, what?" My voice was shrill with tension. "What do you want, Derek?"

"You, Harper," he repeated, rolling his eyes as if I were stupid. "I want *you*."

"No," I bit out, my voice firm despite the frisson of fear running up my spine.

Derek smiled at me indulgently. "Yes," he countered. "You belong to me."

Quinn stood and came ot my side, her body vibrating with rage. "She's not a possession, you psychopath!"

Derek's gaze didn't waver from mine, but his smile thinned. "A few months away and you're hanging out with the riffraff. It's time to take out the trash."

My heart hammered against my ribcage, but I forced my voice to remain steady. "Let Quinn and Frank go. I'll go with you, just don't hurt them."

"Harper, no!" Quinn hissed.

Derek's eyes gleamed. "How noble. But it's really too late for that, isn't it?" He sighed dramatically. "I can't have them calling the police the moment we leave."

His right hand moved toward his waistband and withdrew a small, matte-black pistol. The sight of it knocked the air from my lungs.

"It's just me and you now, Harper," he said with a wide smile. "No more distractions. No more loose ends."

"Oh my god." The words escaped on a breath. "You *are* a psycho," I breathed in shock.

Derek pointed the gun at Quinn, whose face had gone chalk-white. "Ladies first."

Time slowed to a painful crawl and everything seemed to happen all at once. Quinn's hands choked up on the baseball bat. Derek's finger curled around the trigger. Frank moaned from behind us on the floor.

I turned toward Quinn, taking us both to the floor as a bang echoed through the garage. I swallowed my scream as we tumbled on top of poor Frank, bracing for the impact of a bullet.

It never came.

The ringing faded slowly from my ears and I raised my head to find Quinn's eyes large and round staring back at me. From behind us grunts and exhalations sounded softly.

"Get off me, you horse," Quinn murmured.

I unfroze and rolled to the side, flopping down onto the hard concrete and sitting up. My mouth fell open at the sight of Ronan--in all of his naked glory--pounding his fist into Derek's face.

Quinn sat up beside me. "Holy shit, that's hot," she gasped.

I reached over and slapped a hand over her eyes.

She slouched in disappointment. "No fair."

Derek was trying to fight back, but Ronan was taller, stronger, and faster. Derek threw a punch that landed on Ronan's side but he didn't even flinch. Pulling back his arm, tattooed bicep bulging, Ronan slammed a blow onto Derek's jaw. Derek's eyes rolled back as his knees buckled and he collapsed in a heap on the garage floor.

For a breathless moment, Ronan stood frozen. His broze skin stretched over taut muscles as he waited to see if Derek would stay down.

I knew I should be watching the dangerous man on the floor, but my gaze was snagged by the tight, round muscles of Ronan's ass.

"What's happening?" Quinn groused.

As if she'd broken a spell, Ronan's body sagged and he swayed slightingly. I moved my gaze up to search his face as he turned toward me.

"Are you okay?" He asked, landing awkwardly on his knees before us.

I reluctantly dropped my hand from Quinn's eyes and she stared up at him, her mouth hanging open as her eyes scanned down his body. "Wow. You're really—"

"Bleeding," I gasped, as a dark stain spread across Ronan's bare abdomen. "Oh god, Ronan, you're bleeding!"

He looked down, surprise registering on his face as if he'd only just noticed. "Huh. That's not good."

He lurched forward and I sprang forward to catch him. He was heavy—solid muscle that threatened to take us both down to the concrete. All I could do was guide his fall, arranging him on the floor beside Frank.

"Oh my god," I gasped, my brain starting to work again. "He's been shot."

"Holy shit," Quinn choked out. "What do we do?"

"Call 911," I ordered, pressing my hands to the wound in Ronan's side. Blood seeped between my fingers, warm and slick and terrifyingly abundant.

And then he was gone. A small, worn teddy bear lay limp on the concrete, stuffing flowing from its torn body. White fluff was scattered across the floor, where Ronan's blood had stained the concrete only moments before.

"Harper!" Chief Hudson called from the open doorway, his solid form silhouetted against the bright afternoon light outside.

"We're here," I called in relief, my body sagging over the still bear. "We need an ambulance!"

Quinn knelt beside me, her face ashen. "We can't call an ambulance for a teddy bear!" she hissed.

I took a deep breath, trying to control my racing heart. "Your dad needs an ambulance," I pointed out. I hesitated before continuing. "And Derek."

"Fuck that douchebag," she bit out under her breath as the Chief approached. "He doesn't need an ambulance. He needs a hearse."

<h1 style="text-align:right">Seventeen</h1>

Frank was awake and talking by the time the ambulance arrived. And so was Derek, who sadly did not need a hearse. He sat on the curb outside the garage, his hands cuffed behind his back, as he waited for the second ambulance.

Quinn had gone with Frank to get checked out at the hospital, but she'd left me her baseball bat. *Just in case*, she'd said, giving Derek a significant look before hopping into the ambulance. He did try to speak to me once, but Meredith threatened to shoot him so he just sat there and sulked.

I was oblivious to it all. All of my focus was on the ruined teddy bear sitting in my lap. I'd meticulously gathered every piece of soft, white fluff off of the concrete floor and was gently inserting it back into the ragged hole in his belly. I smoothed out the lumps, my heart constricting as I probed the tear in the little, still body.

A second ambulance arrived for Derek, who was manhandled onto a stretcher and loaded up.

"I want my lawyer," he slurred through what appeared to be a broken jaw.

"Oh, you'll need one," Meredith replied flatly, as she climbed in after him.

At some point, someone had turned on the garage's big overhead lights, which had made it easier to find all of the tiny pieces of Ronan scattered across the floor. My eyes were still searching for any I might have missed when a large shadow fell over me. Chief Hudson stood over me, his weathered face creased with concern.

"Let's get you off the floor, kiddo," he said, offering me a hand up.

I stared at him blankly, cradling the bear's limp form closer.

The Chief squatted down beside me. "The guys need to take pictures, Harper," he said gently. "Let's go sit at Quinn's desk, okay?"

I didn't offer any resistance as he helped me stand. The Chief nodded at the technician from the crime lab, who was measuring the bloodstain on the floor where Frank had been lying, and led me over to Quinn's big, padded spinny chair.

"I'll get you some coffee," the Chief said, moving toward the ancient pot in the corner.

I sank into Quinn's chair, resisting the urge to squeeze the bear. Instead I placed him gently in my lap, holding my palm over his torn body. Tears threatened again, but I took long, deep breaths. When the Chief returned with a steaming mug, I met his gaze.

"Better?" he asked, pulling up a folding metal chair to face mine.

I nodded, taking the coffee. "Yes," I replied firmly.

"Can you tell me what happened?"

I took a fortifying sip and began. "The door was unlocked when we got back from lunch. Frank told us to run back to the diner to get you, but—" I stopped abruptly, my eyes widening in realization. "My phone. I dropped it."

"We have it," the Chief confirmed. "It was sitting on the sidewalk. I got your call, and when you didn't answer, I came to check on you."

Tears stung my eyes again. "Thank you."

The Chief patted my hand. "Looks like you guys had already taken care of business," he smiled but his eyes were concerned, his gaze resting on the bear under our hands.

"We had some help," I confirmed softly.

He nodded. "Tell me everything."

"Move aside, move aside," came a familiar voice, and the crime scene techs who were packing up their equipment fled in what might have been panic as Mrs. Peterson bustled through the garage door. Her velour tracksuit was the same pale pink as her teased updo and her big sequined tote bag glittered under the fluorescent lights.

The Chief stood, offering his chair as she made her way to us. "Ma'am," he greeted her with a nod.

"Bobby," she replied, patting her shellacked hair as she sank gracefully into the folding chair. She drew a small wooden box from her bag, not much bigger than the palm of my hand, and placed it onto Quinn's desk. "I brought you something that you need, Harper."

I gazed at her in confusion. "That's really kind of you, Mrs. Peterson, but I don't think—"

"Something that *Ronan* needs." She leaned forward, her gaze intense.

My eyebrows shot up. "You know about...?" I trailed off, glancing at the Chief.

Mrs. Peterson's laugh tinkled through the garage. "Of course I do, dear." She leaned forward and flipped open the lid of the little wooden box. Inside was a spool of red thread. "How are your sewing skills?"

My brain ticked over slowly, taking way too long to make the connection before her meaning clicked. I tore my gaze away from the brilliant red of the thread. My palm still rested over the tiny bear's belly. I lifted my hand slowly, holding my breath.

There was no blood, no gushing wound. There was just a small tear in the bear's fur, a tuft of white fluff peaking out.

My breath escaped on a puff of air and I met Mrs. Peterson's gaze squarely. "I can do this."

Her answering smile was brilliant. "Of course you can, my dear."

Mrs. Peterson plucked the spool of thread from the box. The thread was a bright, true red and appeared to be a heavy weight cotton. The spool itself was old fashioned and made of wood. She unwound a length of the thread, snipping it off with tiny scissors pulled from the depths of her sequined bag. She produced a large, shiny needle, easily the length of my finger, from somewhere and expertly threaded it on the first try.

"For you, my dear," she announced, holding out the threaded needle.

I pinched the cool metal between my thumb and forefinger and held her gaze for a moment. "Thank you, Mrs. Peterson."

"You're the one doing the work." She waved away my gratitude and settled back in her seat, turning to face the Chief as I steadied myself for the task at hand. There was no obvious top or bottom to the hole, so I chose an arbitrary spot to begin.

"And you'll make sure that awful Derek fellow doesn't bother Harper or Ronan again. Won't you, Bobby?" Mrs. Peterson eyed the Chief with a raised eyebrow.

The Chief nodded meekly. "Yes, ma'am."

I let their conversation wash over me and took a deep breath. Holding it in, I pushed the sharp tip of the long needle through the fuzzy material of the bear's belly, angling it to come up on the other side of the wound.

One stitch down.

In the end I placed ten not-quite-perfect stitches across the tear. The moment of truth came as I pulled on the end of the thread and the lines disappeared, one by one, as the hole zipped closed. I ran my thumb over the faint seam, amazed at how good the repair looked. I tied a knot as close as I could to the fabric.

Mrs. Peterson's tiny scissors appeared in my peripheral vision and I shot her a smile. Taking the scissors, I clipped off the end of the thread and handed the scissors and the needle back to her with another, "Thank you."

"That looks lovely, my dear," she said gently, resting her hand over mine for a moment. "Now the rest is up to him."

The sun was setting by the time the Chief dropped me off at the door to my tiny cottage. It took a lot of convincing to get him to leave me alone, but Derek was in custody and the danger had passed.

"We have him dead to rights," the Chief began with a soft expression as we stood on the porch of my little cottage. "But if it goes to court..." He let the words trail off.

"I'll testify," I told him firmly, meeting his gaze.

The tension around his eyes melted into deep smile lines and he patted me on the shoulder. He still waited outside my door until I locked it, but finally I was able to sit on my couch and have a small nervous breakdown.

I let myself blubber for about thirty minutes, and then wiped away my tears, blew my nose, and got up to make myself some dinner. I brought the bear with me into the kitchen, compulsively checking his stitches every few minutes. The repair was nearly invisible, but I could feel the seam when I ran my finger over it.

The bear sat propped up against the toaster as I stirred cheese into noodles and kept up a running commentary.

"I'm making extra," I told him. "Just in case."

There was no answer, but I refused to let myself dwell on the possibility that I might never see Ronan—the real Ronan—ever again.

I moved the bear to the center of my table and was sitting down with a mug full of cheesy noodles when my phone rang. Quinn's name appeared on the screen.

"We're home," she said brightly as soon as I answered the call.

I sagged in relief, feeling some of the tension ease from my shoulders. "Your dad is okay? The hospital didn't want to keep him overnight?"

Quinn chuckled. "Oh no, they totally did," she confirmed. "But he refused. So now I get to wake him up every hour. All. Through. The. Night."

"Fun. What exactly did the doctor say?" I asked, shovelling a spoonful of too-hot noodles into my mouth and then breathing around it.

"Six stitches and a mild concussion," Quinn reported. "But Dad refused to stay for observation because he's a stubborn old goat."

"It was just a bump," Frank grumbled faintly in the background.

"A bump that knocked you out cold for several minutes," Quinn retorted.

"I'm so glad he's okay," I said softly. "I don't know what I would have done if—"

"Dad is fine," Quinn interrupted firmly. "And Douchebag Derek's sorry ass is in jail, where it belongs."

I lowered my spoon into the mug and rubbed a hand over my eyes. "I'm so sorry, Quinn. Please let your dad know I never intended to bring this kind of trouble to you guys."

"Stop," Quinn said sharply. "You will not take responsibility for Derek being a psycho. That is on him."

"I just don't know how I didn't see it," I admitted softly.

Quinn made a noise that sounded suspiciously like *pshaw*. "What are you, the asshole whisperer? I knew

Derek just as long as you did and I didn't know he was a complete nutbag either."

I just shook my head, having no response to that.

"On a much more important topic," Quinn continued, "Seen any hot naked men lately?"

I barked out a laugh that ended on a suspiciously wet sigh. "Not recently, no," I admitted.

"Well, I'm sure you will," Quinn announced firmly.

"Mrs. Peterson came to the garage and gave me some kind of special red thread to sew up the hole," I told her hesitantly.

"Special thread?" Quinn repeated dubiously.

The bear was sitting before me on the table, its green glass eyes judging me as I murmured, "Magic thread."

There was silence on the other end of the line.

"Do you think I'm crazy?" I asked quietly.

"Yes," Quinn replied without hesitation. "Yes, I do."

We both burst into slightly hysterical laughter.

Eighteen

Ronan

I drifted into awareness slowly, like surfacing from deep water. Something was different. The familiar quiet hum of Harper's house wrapped around me—the gentle ticking of the kitchen clock, the soft whoosh of her breathing beside me, the distant crash of waves against the shore beyond her windows.

But something had changed.

My eyes flew open. Darkness greeted me, broken only by a thin strip of moonlight slicing through the gap in the curtains.

Harper stirred beside me, mumbling something incoherent before settling again. Her hair spilled across the pillow, one arm flung over her head in that way she had when she was deeply asleep.

I sat up carefully, Harper's soft sheets pooling around my waist. I slid from the bed, my bare feet connecting with the cool wooden floor. I padded across the room to the window, pulling back the curtain. The moon hung fat and bright in the sky, casting silver light across the quiet yard. I pressed my palm flat against the glass, feeling the smoothness against my skin.

Minutes ticked by.

My reflection stared back at me from the window—a naked man with wild hair and wilder eyes. My hand drifted to my stomach, fingers tracing the faint ridge of a scar where the bullet had torn through me. Where Harper had stitched me back together.

Something was different.

I slid back under the covers, propping myself on one elbow to watch her sleep. A strand of hair had fallen across her face, and I gently tucked it behind her ear, marveling at the softness of her skin beneath my finger-tips.

"Hey, sweetheart," I murmured, leaning down to press a gentle kiss to her forehead. "Wake up."

She scrunched her nose adorably but didn't open her eyes.

I chuckled, trailing my fingers down her cheek. "Harper," I whispered against her ear. "I've got a surprise for you."

Her eyelids fluttered. "Mmm?" she mumbled.

I captured her lips with mine, a soft, sweet kiss that lingered. Her lips were warm and pliant beneath mine, still heavy with sleep.

Then she stiffened, her eyes flying open.

"Ronan?" Her voice was barely a breath.

"Hi," I said softly.

Harper launched herself at me, her arms wrapping around my neck with enough force to knock me onto my back. Her face pressed into my neck, and I felt hot tears against my skin.

"You're alive," she choked out between sobs. "You're really alive."

I wrapped my arms around her, holding her tight against my chest. "I'm alive," I confirmed, my own voice rough with emotion. "And I think I'm here to stay."

She pulled back just enough to see my face, her hazel eyes swimming with tears in the moonlight. "How do you know?"

"I just do," I replied, reaching up to wipe away a tear from her cheek with my thumb. "Something's different. I can feel it."

Harper's hands cupped my face, her thumbs sweeping over my cheekbones as if memorizing my features. Then she was kissing me—desperate, hungry kisses that tasted of salt and relief and love.

I returned her kisses with equal fervor, my hands sliding up her back beneath her thin sleep shirt. Her skin was impossibly soft and warm beneath my palms.

When we finally broke apart, both breathing heavily, I rested my forehead against hers.

"I missed you," she whispered.

My heart clenched. "I'm so sorry, sweetheart. I heard you. I just couldn't—"

She silenced me with a fierce kiss. "Don't you dare apologize. You saved my life. You saved Frank and Quinn."

I smoothed her hair back from her forehead, drinking in the sight of her tear-streaked face illuminated by moonlight. "Worth it," I said simply.

Harper laughed through her tears, the sound like music. "You are such a hero cliché."

"Only for you," I promised, pressing a kiss to the corner of her mouth. "Always for you."

Her smile faded, replaced by something more serious. "Are you really staying? For good?"

I nodded, sliding my hands down to rest at her waist. "I think so," I told her. "It feels different this time."

Fresh tears spilled down her cheeks, but she was smiling again—a radiant, hopeful smile that made my chest ache.

"Harper Brinkman," I began, my voice suddenly rough. "I've been alive for over three quarters of a century, and I've never met anyone like you. I've watched the world change from behind glass, seen technology evolve and fashions come and go. But you—you're timeless and perfect and everything I never knew I needed."

Her breath hitched, but she didn't interrupt.

"I want to spend whatever life I have left with you. Building engines, rebuilding classics, making you breakfast, and making you smile." My hands tightened at her waist. "If you'll have me."

Harper's answer was another searing kiss, her hands threading through my hair as she pressed herself against me. When she finally pulled back, her eyes were bright with tears and something far warmer.

"I'm going to take that as a yes," I murmured against her lips.

"Yes," she confirmed with a watery laugh. "So much yes."

Her hands wandered over my chest, tracing the contours of muscle as if relearning me. "I was so afraid you weren't coming back," she admitted quietly.

"Wild horses couldn't keep me away," I promised, my own hands slipping beneath her shirt again, this time sliding upward to brush the underside of her breasts. "Or bullets. Or crazy ex-boyfriends."

Harper shivered under my touch, her back arching slightly. "Don't joke about that," she admonished, but there was no heat in her words.

"Sorry," I whispered, capturing her mouth again in a slower, deeper kiss.

Her sleep shirt bunched around her waist as my hands explored her skin. The silky texture of it, the warmth, the subtle curves and valleys—I wanted to map every inch, to memorize her body with my hands and mouth.

"Too many clothes," I murmured against her lips.

She laughed softly, sitting up to straddle my hips before pulling her shirt over her head in one fluid motion. Moonlight painted her skin silver, turning her into a goddess glowing against the darkness.

"You are so goddamn beautiful," I breathed, reaching up to cup her breasts.

Harper leaned into my touch, her eyes fluttering closed as my thumbs brushed over her nipples. "And you," she said, her voice breathy, "are still the hottest man I've ever seen."

"Even with the scar?" I asked, guiding her hand to the mark on my stomach.

Her fingers traced it gently, reverently. "Especially with the scar," she insisted.

I sat up, wrapping an arm around her waist to keep her in my lap. Our bare chests pressed together, skin to skin, and I buried my face in the crook of her neck, inhaling her scent—lavender and motor oil and something uniquely Harper.

Harper's hands tangled in my hair, holding me against her as she ground her hips against mine. Even through the thin cotton of her shorts, the friction was enough to make me groan.

"I need you," she whispered against my ear. "Now."

I slid my hands beneath the waistband of her shorts, finding her already slick and ready. "These need to go," I murmured, tugging at the fabric between us.

Harper lifted herself just enough for me to push her shorts down her thighs. She kicked them off impatiently before settling back in my lap, now gloriously naked.

"Much better," I approved, my hands spanning her waist.

She smiled against my lips, reaching between us to guide me into position. "Stop talking," she ordered softly.

And then she was sinking down onto me, enveloping me in tight, wet heat that had my eyes rolling back and my fingers digging into her hips. We both groaned at the sensation of being connected again after what felt like an eternity apart.

"Good?" I managed to ask through gritted teeth.

Harper nodded, her forehead pressed against mine as she adjusted to the fullness. "So good," she breathed, rolling her hips experimentally.

I tightened my grip on her waist, helping her find a rhythm that had us both gasping. She moved like liquid moonlight above me, her hair falling forward to create a curtain around our faces.

"I love you," I whispered against her lips. "I love you so damn much."

"I love you too," she responded, her voice breaking on a moan as I shifted the angle slightly.

We moved together, climbing higher and higher, our bodies remembering each other despite our time apart. Her hands clutched at my shoulders, nails digging into my skin as her pace quickened.

"Ronan," she gasped, her body beginning to tremble. "I'm close—"

"Let go," I urged, sliding one hand between us to where we were joined. "I've got you."

The moment my fingers found her center, Harper shattered. Her body clenched around mine, her back arching as she cried out my name. The sight of her coming undone pushed me over the edge, and I followed her into bliss, holding her tight against me as waves of pleasure washed through us both.

As our breathing gradually slowed, Harper collapsed against my chest, her face tucked into the crook of my neck. I stroked my hand down her spine, savoring the weight of her in my arms.

"That was..." she trailed off, apparently lost for words.

"Yeah," I agreed with a soft laugh. "It definitely was."

We stayed like that for several minutes, neither of us willing to move. Finally, Harper shifted, disconnecting our bodies with a small sound of protest before curling against my side.

I pulled the sheets over us both, tucking her closer against me. Her hair tickled my chin, and I pressed a kiss to the top of her head.

"Promise me something?" she asked, her voice already thick with approaching sleep.

"Anything," I replied without hesitation.

"Promise you'll still be here when I wake up." Her words were muffled against my chest, but the vulnerability in them pierced my heart.

I tightened my arm around her. "Harper Brinkman, wild bears couldn't drag me away,"

Nineteen

Harper

"What's the verdict, Doc?" Mrs. Campbell asked as I leaned over the engine of her ancient Cadillac, her weathered hands clutching her oversized purse like it might make a break for it.

"Well, it's not terminal," I assured her with a smile, wiping my hands on a shop rag. "Just needs a good tune-up."

Behind me, the garage door rolled up with a metallic rattle, and a familiar rumble made my heart skip a beat. I turned to see Ronan backing a coupe into the service bay, raindrops glistening on its hood.

He killed the engine and swung open the door. Our eyes met and I sighed. His slow smile still sent tingles all the way down to my toes.

"Hey, boss," he called, striding toward me with that confident swagger I'd come to adore. "How's Mrs. Campbell's Caddy?"

"It could use a little TLC if you're up for it," I replied, fighting the urge to wipe the smudge of grease off my cheek.

Mrs. Campbell's rheumy eyes darted between us, a knowing smile spreading across her face. "You two are just precious," she cooed. "Reminds me of me and my Harold, back in the day."

My cheeks burned. One month of being officially together, and I still blushed like a middle schooler whenever someone commented on our relationship.

"We'll have your car ready by Friday, Mrs. Campbell," I promised, steering the conversation back to safer ground.

"No rush, my dear," she patted my arm. "I know you've been busy since Frank retired and you and Quinn took over the garage."

I escaped to the bathroom after Mrs. Campbell finally left, scrubbing the worst of the grime from my hands and face. The woman in the mirror looked happier than she had in years—cheeks flushed, eyes bright, hair escaping the ponytail in wild tendrils.

When I returned, Ronan was waiting with a steaming mug of coffee.

"Thought you could use this," he said, handing me the cup. His fingers brushed mine, warm and solid.

I took a grateful sip, the rich flavor washing away the smell of motor oil. "Thanks," I sighed in happiness.

Quinn appeared beside us, clipboard in hand. "If you two lovebirds are done making googly eyes at each other, we've got Chief Hudson pulling in."

Sure enough, the Chief's cruiser was easing into the open garage door, its bulk somehow managing to look both menacing and friendly at the same time.

The Chief excited his car, his uniform crisp, despite the wet day. He nodded at me and Quinn before his gaze settled on Ronan.

"Got your paperwork, son," he announced, patting the manila envelope tucked under his arm. "Social security card, birth certificate, and driver's license."

My breath caught. After weeks of calling in favors and navigating bureaucratic tangles, Ronan O'Neill was officially alive again, this time with a birthdate that didn't make him eligible for senior citizen discounts.

"Age twenty-seven," the Chief continued, handing over the envelope. "Clean record, though I was tempted to throw in a jaywalking citation just to make it look authentic."

Ronan laughed, the sound deep and warm as he accepted the envelope. "I owe you one, Chief."

The older man waved him off. "How's Frank doing?" the Chief asked Quinn, changing the subject.

Quinn brightened. "He's definitely enjoying his retirement. If you stop by the house, he's got a freezer full of fish he'll pawn off on you."

"Tell him poker night's still on for Thursday," the Chief said. "And he can bring as much of that fish as he wants. I may be joining him on his next trip."

After the Chief left, I turned to find Ronan staring at his new ID, running his thumb over the laminated surface.

"Everything okay?" I asked quietly.

He looked up, a strange mix of emotions crossing his face. "It's weird," he admitted. "Having proof that I exist again."

As if conjured by his memories, a 1972 Triumph rolled into the garage. Lenny brought the bike to a stop in the center of the shop and dismounted. He removed his helmet and brushed off the damp shoulders of his leather jacket.

Ronan approached, hand outstretched. "Hey, Lenny! Is there a problem with the Triumph?"

Lenny grabbed Ronan's hand and gave it a pump. "Nah, it's perfect, as always." He unzipped his jacket and pulled an envelope from inside. "I heard through the grapevine that you're all legal and stuff now."

Ronan smiled, his face split with joy. "News travels fast in this town."

"Yup." Lenny thrust the envelope forward. "So I figured it was time. This belongs to you, Ronan. Always has."

Ronan opened the envelope and pulled out a folded sheet of paper. His expression shifted from confusion to disbelief.

"The Triumph?" he whispered. "You're giving me the bike?"

Lenny shrugged, suddenly fascinated by his shoelaces. "Technically it was always yours. I was just keeping it warm."

"Lenny," Ronan's voice was rough with emotion. "I don't know what to say."

"You can say you'll bring it to the convention next year." Lenny fidgeted with his glasses. "There are a whole lot of people who would really love to meet you."

Ronan laughed, clapping Lenny on the shoulder. "I'd love to, man. Thank you."

He rocked on his feet as Lenny swept him into a hug, his eyes dancing as they met mine over Lenny's shoulder.

After Lenny left, practically floating with excitement, I raised an eyebrow at Ronan. "You're going to be his star attraction."

"Small price to pay," Ronan replied, jingling the keys in his palm. "This bike was my pride and joy."

"And now it's yours again," I said, wrapping my arms around his waist and inhaling the familiar scent of leather and motor oil that clung to him. "Ronan O'Neill, age twenty-seven, exists on paper, has a home, a job—"

"A gorgeous girlfriend," he added, kissing the top of my head.

"—and now his vintage motorcycle back," I finished. "Not bad for a guy who spent the last fifty years as a stuffed animal."

Quinn cleared her throat loudly from behind the counter. "If you're done with your Hallmark moment, we've got actual paying customers waiting, *partner*."

I stuck my tongue out at her, but reluctantly pulled away from Ronan. "Duty calls."

The afternoon passed in a blur of oil changes and brake pad replacements. By closing time, my muscles ached pleasantly from a day of honest work, and the afternoon sun cast golden light through the garage windows.

Quinn leaned against my workbench with a dramatic sigh. "God, your life is so boring now."

I looked up from where I was organizing my tools. "I'm sorry?"

"You heard me." She grinned, twirling a strand of red hair around her finger. "No more death-defying rescues, no more magical transformations, no more psycho ex-boyfriends trying to kidnap you."

"And that's bad?"

Quinn shrugged. "You go to work, you go home, you make dinner with your hunky boyfriend, you fix old cars in your garage. It's like you're living in some small-town rom-com epilogue."

I wiped my hands on a shop rag and considered her words. Was my life boring now? A month ago, I'd been sleeping with a wrench under my pillow, jumping at shadows. Now I slept soundly in Ronan's arms.

My gaze moved to the far side of the garage where Ronan was sliding out from under a pickup truck. He rose to his full height, stretching his arms over his shoulders as the afternoon sunlight played over his bronze skin.

As if he felt the weight of my stare, he glanced up and our eyes met. A smile stretched across his face, crinkling at the corners of his eyes.

"If this is boring," I said finally, "I'll take it."

Epilogue

Agatha

"Another day, another dollar," I muttered, flicking the switch to bathe the diner in darkness save for the soft green glow of the exit sign. The ceiling fans sighed in response, spinning down from the day's labor.

My apartment waited upstairs—a cozy little nest above the diner with a DVR full of cooking shows and a pint of rocky road with my name on it. But something about the night called to me. Through the large glass window that stretched across the front of the diner, the moonlight was shockingly bright, creating a path of silver along the deserted street that beckoned.

I slipped outside into the moonlight and locked the diner door behind me, testing the handle three times. The cool salt air kissed my cheeks, washing away the lingering scent of fryer oil that perpetually clung to my clothes and hair. Stars winked overhead, unobscured by the off-season darkness of Santa Paola's boardwalk.

My kingdom might be inside those walls, but tonight the ocean called my name. Two blocks over and one block down and the wooden planks of the boardwalk creaked beneath my sneakers.

Just like the streets of Santa Paola, the boardwalk was deserted. The sunseekers were long gone and I had officially survived my first tourist season running the diner solo. Mom and Dad's updates from the retirement community arrived weekly, each one featuring increasingly alarming photos of them doing water aerobics or driving golf carts with wild abandon. The latest showed Dad wearing a Hawaiian shirt so loud it could probably direct air traffic.

"They're not even missing this place," I whispered to the night air, a smile tugging at my mouth.

The ocean rumbled its steady rhythm to my right, crashing against the shore in lazy, hypnotic succession. To my left, the shuttered carnival games and food stands stood like sleeping sentinels. My sneakers scuffed against a patch of sticky taffy residue—a relic from the summer tourists.

A laminated poster fluttered against the freestanding community notice board at the edge of the sidewalk, its neon yellow garish even in the moonlight. I squinted at the bold lettering: KITCHEN COMBAT: SANTA PAOLA'S ULTIMATE RESTAURANT WAR.

"Well, hello there," I murmured, stepping closer. My finger traced the details: competition held over the two weekends of the Santa Paola Fair, judged by celebrity chefs, grand prize ten thousand dollars and a feature in Coastal Cuisine magazine.

The deadline for entry was tomorrow.

"Agatha Riley, Queen of Kitchen Combat," I tried out loud. "Has a nice ring to it."

My mind raced with possibilities as I unpinned the poster from the board. I could make my mom's secret recipe cinnamon rolls. Or the maple bacon cheesecake that caused a minor riot last summer when we ran out. Or the chili that had even the local fishermen weeping with joy.

"You've got this," I told myself firmly, tucking the rolled up poster into my jacket. "Time to show Santa Paola what—"

A metallic screech pierced the night air, followed by a muffled curse. I ducked instinctively behind the bulletin board, heart hammering.

Peering around the edge, I spotted two figures huddled around an ancient claw machine. One held a flashlight while the other wielded what appeared to be...a jackhammer?

"Let's try the side panel again." a deep voice whispered, low and frustrated.

The flashlight bobbed as its holder shifted position. "Don't damage the bears," came a softer reply, a woman's voice.

The woman moved into the spill of moonlight, and I recognized Harper Brinkman's profile. Which meant the man must be her mysterious new boyfriend.

"What the hell?" I breathed, watching as Harper handed him a different tool—a crowbar, from the looks of it.

"Easy, Ronan," Harper cautioned as he wedged it against the machine's frame. "We just need to create enough space to reach in."

The crowbar slipped with a harsh clang against the metal casing. Ronan cursed again, this time more colorfully.

"Maybe we need a different approach," Harper suggested, rubbing his arm. "We could try to pick the lock instead of forcing it."

Ronan stepped back, running a hand through his dark hair. "There has to be a way," he insisted, his voice tight with emotion. "They're right there, Harper."

In the claw machine? I pressed myself flatter against the bulletin board. Clearly, I was witnessing something strange, even by Santa Paola standards.

Harper touched his face gently. "We'll get them out, I promise. But maybe not tonight."

Ronan slid down to sit with his back against the machine, his face a mask of defeat in the moonlight. Harper knelt beside him, taking his hands in hers. "This isn't your fault."

Ronan leaned his forehead against hers. "What would I do without you?"

He pulled her closer, his arms encircling her as he buried his face in her hair. "I love you," he murmured, just loud enough for me to hear.

"I love you too," Harper replied, and the simple, honest declaration struck a chord deep in my chest.

I turned away from their embrace, a sudden intruder in their private moment. A heaviness settled in my stomach—not quite envy, but a recognition of something I didn't have. Running the diner filled my days with purpose and people, but my nights remained stubbornly solitary.

"Focus on the competition, Agatha," I whispered to myself, squaring my shoulders. "That's what you need right now."

As I took a step away, something glinted in the moonlight at my feet—a flash of copper against the weathered wood. I bent down, my fingers closing around a large coin.

It was warm to the touch, almost vibrating with energy. Holding it up to catch the moonlight, I saw an embossed eye in the center, surrounded by block lettering:

YOUR ADVENTURE
AWAITS

Read Agatha and Bruno's adventure in Bearly Enough, coming soon on Amazon!

Want to know how it all began? Read Ronan's story in Bearly Alive, 1975 for free today by signing up for Ferguson Ray's newsletter!

About the author

Ferguson Ray is a pseudonym for a woman named Michael, whose parents should never be allowed to name anything, Michael is a teacher, an artist, and a certified Crazy Dog Lady. Michael lives in an old yellow farmhouse near the sea where she writes books and snuggles dogs all day long. You can find her work at http://PepperbackPress.com.

Want more?
@pepperbackpress